I0763157

OFF-LIMITS DOC ON DECK

LUANA DaROSA

If you purchased this book without a cover you should be aware that this book is stolen property. It was reported as "unsold and destroyed" to the publisher, and neither the author nor the publisher has received any payment for this "stripped book."

PLEASE RECYCLE • THIS PRODUCT IS RECYCLABLE •

Recycling programs for this product may not exist in your area

ISBN-13: 978-1-335-99368-7

Off-Limits Doc on Deck

Copyright © 2026 by Luana DaRosa

All rights reserved. No part of this book may be used or reproduced in any manner whatsoever without written permission.

Without limiting the exclusive rights of any author, contributor or the publisher of this publication, any unauthorized use of this publication to train generative artificial intelligence (AI) technologies is expressly prohibited. Harlequin also exercises their rights under Article 4(3) of the Digital Single Market Directive 2019/790 and expressly reserves this publication from the text and data mining exception.

This is a work of fiction. Names, characters, places and incidents are either the product of the author's imagination or are used fictitiously. Any resemblance to actual persons, living or dead, businesses, companies, events or locales is entirely coincidental.

For questions and comments about the quality of this book, please contact us at CustomerService@Harlequin.com.

TM and ® are trademarks of Harlequin Enterprises ULC.

Harlequin Enterprises ULC
22 Adelaide St. West, 41st Floor
Toronto, Ontario M5H 4E3, Canada
www.Harlequin.com

HarperCollins Publishers
Macken House, 39/40 Mayor Street Uppe
Dublin 1, D01 C9W8, Ireland
www.HarperCollins.com

Printed in U.S.A.

1 2 3 4 5 6 7 8 9 10 HDC 28 27 26 25

Cat entered the room and stopped dead. A laugh—almost a bark—escaped her.

"You have got to be kidding me."

There it stood just the way Theo remembered from when he'd got in here a few hours ago: the single, queen-size bed jammed up against the far wall.

Catalina whirled around, eyes narrowed on him just as he entered. "Did you do this?" she asked, and he couldn't swallow the incredulous snort.

"Yes, of course I planned this. When Amelie begged me to sub in for her, I thought to myself: *You know what would make this whole thing even more* fun? *Sleeping in the same bed as my sister's best friend.*"

"So...are we going to fight over it?" Catalina asked, her voice loud in the small space. "Or is this one of those free-for-alls where we both pretend not to care and then one of us cracks and sleeps on the floor?"

"We could implement a schedule. Two-hour shifts, alternating horizontal and vertical positions, strictly back-to-back. Minimal contact guaranteed."

Dear Reader,

Thank you for picking up *Off-Limits Doc on Deck*. I got to have so much fun with this one, putting clues about my own life and experiences all over it.

As the middle child in a loud family, I thought we needed our happily-ever-afters, and that's where the idea of Catalina arrived. A competent woman struggling to find her place in the world because she's so used to handling everyone else's wishes without ever looking to her own. Now, my family wasn't nearly as dramatic—and that's totally me saying this and not my mum forcing me to put this in here.

I also have a soft spot (okay, a full-blown obsession) with the kind of hero who's been quietly in love for years. The kind who watches, waits and would do anything to keep the heroine safe—even if it means keeping his feelings under wraps. Enter Theo, our grumpy, brooding doctor who's always had a thing for his sister's best friend.

And finally: the cruise. While writing, I lived vicariously through Cat and Theo—sipping cocktails on sun-drenched decks, dancing under stars and falling in love somewhere between Sicily and Athens.

With love,

Luana

Once at home in sunny Brazil, **Luana DaRosa** has since lived on three different continents, though her favorite romantic location remains the tropical places of Latin America. When she's not typing away at her latest romance novel or reading about love, Luana is either crocheting, buying yarn she doesn't need or chasing her bunnies around her house. She lives with her partner in a cozy town in the south of England. Find her on X under the handle @ludarosabooks.

Books by Luana DaRosa

Harlequin Medical Romance

Amazon River Vets

The Vet's Convenient Bride
The Secret She Kept from Dr. Delgado

Buenos Aires Docs

Surgeon's Brooding Brazilian Rival

Valentine Flings

Hot Nights with the Arctic Doc

Her Secret Rio Baby
Falling Again for the Brazilian Doc
A Therapy Pup to Reunite Them
Pregnancy Surprise with the Greek Surgeon
Falling for Her Miami Rival
Faking It with the Doctor Prince
Falling for the GP Next Door

Visit the Author Profile page at Harlequin.com.

CHAPTER ONE

Day One, Naples

'YOU ARE BY far the worst best friend I've ever had.' In Catalina's mind, it was a fair assessment to lob at Amelie Morgan, her—soon-to-be-former—best friend since medical school. She narrowed her eyes in a glare to make sure the message came across.

From the screen of her phone, Amelie looked up at her with huge eyes and a frown so devastating it looked more cartoon than human.

'Cat, I'm sorry! You know I wanted to be there with you, but I can't get on a cruise ship like this.' She lifted her leg into view of the camera, showing off the cast on her leg.

'Again, why did you think riding a horse for the first time was a good idea right before shipping out on a cruise?' She pushed down on the twinge of guilt in her chest threatening to replace her anger.

Catalina hadn't been there when the accident

happened a few days ago. They'd finished their internships a few weeks ago at Alexander Attano Memorial, and while Catalina had gone back to visit her family in the Dominican Republic, Amelie had apparently decided she'd always wanted to be a show jumper.

Though bearing in mind how aggravating—as usual—her visit home had been, she wasn't sure she wouldn't trade places with her best friend despite the injury. She'd take anything to avoid her family.

'You know my parents didn't let me do anything adventurous when I was younger. Growing up, it was always "study this, grades that". And it's not like we had any time to do fun stuff during med school or in our internship year.' Amelie let out a dramatic sigh, sinking back into the mountain of pillows Catalina could see she was propped up against.

'You get a piercing or an ill-advised tattoo if you have these urges. What you don't do is pretend to be an experienced rider and fall off a horse.' She understood wanting to have fun. Hell, the reason she was weaving through a crowded port in Naples was that they'd decided joining a cruise as working crew would be fun.

Now Catalina was going solo. No, not true. She *wished* she were on her own. But instead—

'*Your brother?* Of all people, your replacement is Theodore?' She knew complaining to Amelie was a mistake. The two siblings were day and night but somehow still thick as thieves. How they got along as well as they did was a mystery for the ages. Like when you tried to plug in a USB thing it was somehow always the wrong way around twice.

It made no sense to think about it because her brain would simply fold in on itself.

Where her best friend was bright and bubbly and over the top, her brother was a surly, broody hunk. That a man this strait-laced was also one of the most beautiful people she'd ever met was no doubt some cosmic joke. The powers that be had looked at Catalina specifically and thought, *On top of middle child syndrome and hyper-competitiveness, let's also give her a hot best friend with an even hotter older brother. But said older brother looks at her like she's gum on his shoe. Oh, and let's make her a virgin. What a lark!*

Amelie covered her face with her free hand, and Catalina thought she caught the flash of a grin. It only deepened her scowl. 'I didn't know what to do, Cat. They told me I needed to find someone else or pay a fine since they are required to have a certain level of staffing. Nautical law or something like that.'

Catalina raised an eyebrow. 'Maritime law?'

'Pretty sure it's nautical law. But whatever, it doesn't matter. I'm really sorry I can't go, but Theo also needed to get busy again, so it's not the worst timing. He's been living the hermit life for too long.' Amelie pulled a face. 'He's grown a beard!'

A flash of heat pulsed through Catalina, bright and quick and gone before she could dwell on the picture of a bearded Theo.

Some of Catalina's annoyance fell away, giving way to a tiny spark of sympathy. Not too much, considering who they were talking about. She'd heard of Theo's burnout and his subsequent quitting as the head of emergency medicine at Morgan Greywater Institute—his family's hospital. *His* hospital.

Everyone had heard of it. Or at least everyone who had even a tiny interest in the goings-on of the medical world. Morgan Greywater was the hospital group at the forefront of medical science and innovation. Whenever any new technique was pioneered or any breakthrough got announced, chances were high it came from Morgan Greywater.

And Theo had been raised to carry the family legacy forward, according to Amelie. Even though she'd gone into medicine, just as their parents had expected their children to, Amelie had soon discovered she wasn't about the legacy life. Instead of doing her internship at the family hospital, she'd chosen to go to the same hospital as Catalina, and so they'd spent the last year living together in Chicago.

'Maybe you can convince him to shave it. It's not a good look on him.' Amelie shook her head. 'But just like…ignore him. You're not the only two people on the medical crew.'

'Avoid each other? Amelie, we booked *one* cabin. I'm stuck in a cabin with your *brother*.' The thought was so outlandish, renewed waves of heat flooded through her. Clearly her body was rebelling against the idea.

'Oh, right…' Wait, Amelie hadn't considered that when she'd asked Theo to sub in for her? 'But it was two beds, right?'

'I sure hope so. Otherwise, your brother is going to sleep on the floor.' The surrounding noise grew louder as more people arrived at the port. Catalina followed the path signposting check-in for any staff. The queue grew longer as she stood there, glaring down at her phone.

'There you go. I knew you'd have a plan. Put up a privacy curtain, and you won't even know he's there. I promise you. As kids, I would randomly poke him for a sign of life because he was so quiet.' A small smile spread over Amelie's lips at the fond memory, and Catalina reminded herself to remain annoyed at her best friend even as her heart softened.

She didn't have memories like that about her seven siblings. Or maybe she did, but they were buried beneath far too complex dynamics for her to recall. Whenever she recalled them now, all she could think about was how she and her older siblings had been wrapped up in an unhealthy rivalry around who could get the most attention from their parents. And how she'd *become* the parent to her younger siblings when no one else stepped up for them.

Catalina pushed the thoughts away.

'Look, why don't you get on board and see how it goes? You might even have fun.'

'Doubtful.' Catalina blew out a breath. 'But at least I have access to the ship's pharmaceutical stash. If I can't stand him, I'll just give myself a sedative for the next three weeks.'

'That's the spirit.' Amelie's laugh sounded more genuine than before, and despite her resolve to stay mad, Catalina felt a glimmer of excitement. She had been looking forward to the cruise for so long and couldn't quite quash the anticipation bubbling beneath her reluctant acceptance.

Thanks to a last-minute dropout from the regular staff roster—and Amelie's countless connections in the medical world—they'd been able to get a contract for the duration of this one cruise. Without a plan on what to do next in her professional life, spending some time exploring the most beautiful parts of Europe while still keeping her skills somewhat honed seemed like the perfect opportunity.

In a life mainly lived to impress others—her parents, tutors, siblings—this was the first thing she was doing just for herself. Not even her best friend's grumpy older brother, who she'd inexplicably had a small crush on since the day they'd met, even though he'd shown literally no interest in her.

'Fine. Getting on the ship now—I'll talk to you later.'

'Love ya, Cat. It'll be great!'

She hung up and shoved her phone into her backpack, as if the act could physically silence the echo of Amelie's optimism. The line in front of her crawled forward, punctuated by the chatter of fellow crew. And even though Amelie wasn't here—and her stupid, sexy brother Theo *was*—Catalina reminded herself that this was *her* time. Her opportunity to let go and find herself outside of work so that the idea of finding her next steps in her career didn't feel so daunting. Find out who she was outside of her role as the middle child of a huge family, always vying for attention by performing even though she knew she wasn't ever going to get the praise she coveted.

Finally see the world with her own eyes instead of living vicariously through the hundreds of travel influencers she followed on Instagram.

Because doing things because they were the *right* things to do hadn't got her any closer to getting acknowledged. Not even after she'd spent years—and hundreds of thousands of dollars—going to med school, thinking that surely with those two letters at the end of her name, she'd get some acknowledgement from her parents. She still remembered the day when she'd shown them her medical licence. *Catalina Reyes, MD.* She also remembered the silence that had followed. And the rather affected 'Good job, *mija*,' before her mother went on to tell Catalina about her sister Sonya and how she was pregnant again.

Twenty-six years she'd tried to impress her parents, get them to tell her how proud they were of her. How well she'd done to carve her own way without help from the family. And what did she have to show for it? She was a whole-ass adult—a *doctor*, for crying out loud—and she was still a virgin. She also had no idea what she wanted to do with her life professionally, but that was a problem she would tackle after the cruise.

This cruise was supposed to be her chance to change her personal life. To stop performing and start living. To let go, maybe hook up with someone hot and emotionally unavailable, and finally close the chapter on her overachiever virgin era. But without Amelie there to play distraction and hype woman, and with Theodore 'fun sponge' Morgan as her new roommate, the odds weren't exactly in her favour.

The thought of Theo sent a nervous jitter through her, and Catalina ignored it, opting to stare at the sleek white hull of the ship as it appeared before her like a promise.

Who cared if Amelie wasn't here? She could do this, right? Could have some no-strings-attached fun? Learn how to live like the rest of the population, who weren't constantly wondering if they were doing their parents proud. Craving the attention and never getting it no matter what.

Shaking those thoughts off, Catalina gripped the handle of her suitcase more tightly as she approached the check-in area. So what if Amelie wasn't here? She could do this on her own. Not a big deal. Like, at all. Right?

'Welcome to *The Aurelian*!' a bright-eyed receptionist greeted Catalina when she stepped into the little foyer somewhere in the lower half of the ship. The name tag read *Sam, they/them* and their smile set Catalina at ease. Well, kind of at ease. There was still the Theo-shaped shadow looming over her, and even though she told herself not to care, her eyes darted around, scanning the face of each crew member as they stepped into the foyer.

He was nowhere to be seen. Bummer. No, wait. Good. Or was it? This entire thing with Theo had her so turned around, Catalina didn't know how to feel. So she pushed it away, focusing on Sam instead.

'Thank you, I'm excited to be here,' she said as she handed her ID over to Sam for them to find her details in the system, wishing for the words to ring true in her mind. She *was* excited, even without Amelie. 'I'm part of the medical crew led by Dr Chen. She sent an email that orientation would be later in the afternoon.' Catalina knew she still had several hours to get settled in, yet she still flicked her wrist to look at her watch as if to confirm time hadn't suddenly skipped ahead.

Sam smiled, their eyes scanning over the screen in front of them. 'Ah, I have you here. Here is your starter package.' They pulled a sleek navy box from behind the desk, the ship's crest stamped in gold foil on the lid.

'Your crew kit. Everyone gets a badge to identify them as crew, a map to the ship for those first few days when it seems labyrinthian, and some coupons for services like the movie theatre and the spa.'

Catalina's eyes went wide, her fingers skating over the crest embossed in the cardboard. Amelie had talked about all the amenities of the ship and what they could do on their days off, but now that she was riding solo she didn't know what to do with any of their plans. Would it be weird to show up on her own for everything? Would she even try?

Between the two, Amelie was the more adventurous one, dragging Catalina along with her regardless of her willingness to participate. But what was the alternative? Sitting in her cabin for three weeks, scrolling through her phone until she knew every corner of the internet? She'd spent so much time on the virgin side of TikTok, figuring out her game plan to finally take that step. Amelie had promised to make herself scarce, but now with Theo…

Heat rushed to Catalina's cheeks at the thought of her involuntary roommate. No chance she would bring anyone to her cabin when *he* would be there. Talk about awkward.

Maybe Amelie had been right. Maybe she could just ignore him. Pretend he was a ghost. A sexy, judging ghost.

'Your room assignment is in there, too. Let me find the key for you,' Sam continued, opening a drawer filled with white keycards sorted alphabetically. When they got to the letter R, they flipped open the pouch and pulled out a few cards, reading the Post-it notes on them before dropping them back in the drawer. 'Strange… I can't find your keycard in here.' Their frown deepened when they looked back up at their screen. 'Oh, right. You are sharing accommodation with someone. Let me check if the cards are under your roommate's name.'

Theo wasn't even here yet and it was already becoming hard to ignore him. She'd been happy to let Amelie handle everything cruise-related, but now that Theo was in the picture she needed to make it clear they were two separate entities.

'We definitely need two keys and receive things in duplicate,' Catalina explained while watching

Sam rifle through the drawer. 'I was supposed to room with someone else, my bestie. But now I'm stuck with her brother, who has this gigantic stick up his—'

A shadow fell over Catalina. One that smelled like expensive sandalwood. A scent that shouldn't feel familiar, and yet… A shiver ran down her spine, and she knew what—who—her senses were warning her of, just as she turned around.

Theodore Morgan was somehow even taller than she remembered, and she had to crane her neck to look up at him. His expression was an unimpressed scowl directed towards her. At this point, she would have thought she'd be immune to his glares since they'd accompanied her through his final year at med school.

But no. Her heart still sped up, almost leaping into her mouth, which was suddenly as dry as a desert. Sweat slicked her palms as Catalina gripped her starter box to her chest.

She should say something, right? Only what? Because the thing she wanted to say—*I hate your sister for sticking me with you*—didn't seem like a good way to start their forced roommate-ship.

Luckily, she didn't have to come up with anything, for Theo said, 'You were saying?'

Catalina blinked several times, the low tone of his voice sending a *zing* through her. Stupid voice. 'I didn't say anything to you.'

'But you were about to say something to Sam.'

He tilted his head to the side, eyes flicking up and down her body—appraising. No, *judging.* The way he always looked at her when they saw each other. 'Something about a stick I have somewhere?'

Heat crept up her neck, flushing into her cheeks. 'Oh, you… How long have you been standing there?' Of course he'd heard her talk trash about him. Why wouldn't he? After all, what would be more hilarious than the man she was forced to share a cabin with standing right behind her when she called him uptight?

The corner of his mouth twitched, and she could practically see the disdain ooze from that little gesture. What had Catalina ever done to him that he held her in such low regard? Yeah, sure, she and Amelie were annoying at times, and could have been considered *obnoxious* in their younger years. But really, wasn't their amusement at him his fault for being so strait-laced?

'Long enough. Came back here because it looked like there were two keys in my envelope.' His hand disappeared into his pocket, and when it came back up he held a white keycard with the ship's branding between his fingers. 'Didn't want my *roommate* to get stuck waiting for me. Despite what she has to say about me.'

Catalina's eyes flared. From the corner of her vision, she could see Sam shuffling on the spot. No doubt that was a first for them, too. Or did colleagues and crewmates often have tense discussions within an hour of boarding?

Before Theo could drag this out any more, Catalina snatched the keycard from his fingers and slapped it on top of her starter box while giving him the best version of a withering glare she could muster. Not that it affected Theo. His mouth remained pressed into a thin line, every twitch in his expression signalling how utterly unimpressed he was with her. Well, he could get in line. Catalina had more than enough experience vying for people's attention and running herself into the ground while doing so.

But that era of her life was over. She was here to choose herself for once. Let go of the incessant need to prove herself to get the attention she'd craved all her life, only for it to be yanked away from her. For the goalposts to move and put her further away from simple acknowledgement.

'Thanks for bringing me my keycard, Theodore. If you don't mind, I will settle in before orientation.' Catalina turned away, taking a steadying breath through her nose, and then shot Theo a look over her shoulder. 'Amelie was right: you look ridiculous with a beard.'

Then she stalked away, as fast as she dared to without giving away how saying that had made her voice wobble. And from behind her, she could have sworn she heard an incredulous laugh.

CHAPTER TWO

Day One, at sea

'AND THAT SHOULD all be sufficient for you to do your jobs. The first shift starts as of right now, and there will be a continuous presence in the med bay until we arrive back here in three weeks' time. You can access your individual shift plan through the app.' Dr Sarah Chen looked around the conference room filled with doctors, nurses and various support staff, then nodded their dismissal.

Theo had already looked around the facilities earlier in the day, having had a quick chat with Dr Chen to introduce himself. During the conversation it had become clear she was aware he was one of *the* Morgans, and so was his sister. Apparently, Amelie hadn't played up that particular fact.

She never did. Unlike himself, his sister had managed to divorce herself from the family name—from the weight attached to it. Even all these years later, he couldn't figure out how she'd done it. How she'd swatted away the expectations of their parents as if they were mere suggestions. As if she hadn't been raised to support a dynasty of medical excellence where failure couldn't be accepted.

Like, for example, facing burnout and quitting the job he'd been raised to do since he was old enough to make memories. Yeah, that hadn't gone over well with his parents, who not only owned the hospital but had also installed him as the head of emergency medicine at Morgan Greywater.

The sound of chairs scraping over the hardwood floor filled the room as people got to their feet. Then soft murmuring followed as people introduced themselves to their new co-workers for the next three weeks. Theo caught the names of the different cities people wanted to visit as they checked the schedule, trying to match their time off to specific stops the ship would take.

He didn't care much about any of this. His presence here was a favour to his sister. One he was coming to regret more the longer he spent on this ship. Which wasn't a good sign, since it had only been a few hours since they'd set sail—could he even say sail when there were none on this ship?—and had left Naples behind.

'Theodore.' A shadow fell over him as he heard his name, and even though he knew the voice—somehow even knew the cadence of the steps—he wasn't prepared to be back in her orbit.

There were a few reasons not to be thrilled. He

was trapped on a floating piece of steel where the preferred way of consuming food was buffet-style—hello, salmonella. His work wasn't exactly what he would call challenging, though that might be a good thing considering he was still recovering from burnout.

But the biggest reason Theo couldn't shake his dark mood had appeared in the form of Dr Catalina Reyes. Ever since they'd met in the lobby, she'd been hovering at the edges of his perception.

'Dr Reyes,' he replied, and got a derisive snort from her in response.

'Really, that's how we're going to do this? Titles?' Her honeyed voice rolled over him, drowning out the noise of the room. One minute into the conversation, and he was already losing his grip on his thoughts. Just as he had when he'd spotted her in the foyer, talking to the receptionist about all the reasons why she hated being near him.

And despite knowing that, he couldn't keep his eyes off Catalina.

'Given we are colleagues now, I thought you'd appreciate some decorum. Or maybe that's not something you're used to from your time at Attano Memorial?' Theo couldn't resist the jibe. Even though his feelings for Morgan Greywater weren't the best ones, the pride in his family's legacy—of his name—was hard to shake.

Spending the last year of med school in close proximity to Catalina, thanks to his sister, he'd learned of her fierce competitiveness, and recognised the signs here as well. She'd spent the entire orientation perched at the front of the room, notes jotted so furiously into her phone it was a wonder the device didn't catch fire.

Given they were on a cruise ship, where most of their patients would have either minor injuries, alcohol-related ailments or the aforementioned food poisoning, he wasn't sure how she planned on channelling her hyper-competitive spirit.

He'd tried not to stare at her throughout Dr Chen's presentation, but it was as if his eyes had developed a will of their own, constantly going back to her in quiet observation.

She'd gathered her coily hair into a puff at the top of her head. It was a practical style but drew his attention to the graceful curve of her neck, the smooth, dark brown skin catching the light. She was wearing a simple white T-shirt, loose but somehow accentuating the lines of her body, and he'd had to force his gaze away before she'd caught him in his silent assessment.

She looked him up and down, frowning. 'You know, when I imagined this cruise, I thought it would be with Amelie. Champagne. Bad decisions. Possibly one good one.' Her eyes dragged over him pointedly. 'Instead, I get Broody McJudgy and a buffet full of norovirus.'

He stared at her, trying not to look amused at the impromptu nickname. Catalina had always had this disarming quality about her, and Theo wasn't about to fall for it now when it hadn't worked on him during their time at med school either.

'You think I'm super excited to be here instead of literally anywhere else?' he asked with more bite than necessary, but it was what came out of his mouth.

When it came to Catalina, he couldn't help himself. The moment he was in her vicinity—since they'd first met in med school—a subtle undercurrent needled at him, demanding all of his attention be on her.

Theo couldn't explain it. He didn't *desire* her. The thought was ridiculous. She was an uninhibited ball of chaos, chasing down opportunities and victories where they didn't exist. A small part of him admired the utter lack of inhibition because it stood in such stark contrast to his own life and how he'd been raised. Always proper, representing the Morgan family, and never allowed to stray for even a moment.

Maybe that was why Amelie had asked him to stay away from her best friend. When she'd asked him to sub in for her here, the warning had struck him. Why had she thought it was necessary to point it out? Now that she was towering over him, pillowy lips downturned and brown eyes pinning him with a combative stare, he felt himself drawn into the challenge he saw in her eyes—even if he didn't understand it.

'No, and I think everyone else can tell you are here against your will. Like, can you try to look a bit less like a hostage and more like a person who had a choice in being here?' Catalina crossed her arms, mouth pressed into a thin line. 'Or is this some burnout thing you still got going on? Amelie warned me about the beard, but I didn't think your personality could get even more sour.'

The prickle of heat Theo had sensed in the back of his neck disappeared as one word rang in his ears. *Burnout*. He shouldn't be surprised Amelie had shared his history with her best friend, yet a part of him had hoped he wouldn't have to explain anything. Come to think of it, why should he explain himself to her? He hadn't asked to be here or to be anywhere near her.

Catalina's eyes widened, her mouth dropping open in an O-shape. 'Sorry, that didn't come out right. I meant—'

Rising to his feet, Theo stuffed his hands into his pockets and shot her his best withering glare over the hammering of his heart. She didn't know. Didn't know how bad it had been at the end, or what it had cost him. She couldn't know because he hadn't told Amelie the whole story either of how he'd crashed out during a shift and had simply never returned to Morgan Greywater.

'Sorry to disappoint,' he said, each word

clipped, and then he turned away from her and walked out of the conference room.

Only apparently Catalina had decided they weren't done yet. The clicking of heels followed him only briefly as the wooden floor gave way to carpet, and he heard her call his name behind him. Then her hand wrapped around his bicep, forcing him to stop if he didn't want to drag her around the ship like a rag doll.

He turned around, looking her up and down, and when he noticed the electric-purple suitcase she was dragging behind her, he paused. Looking back at Catalina, a sheepish smile split her lips.

'What's in your luggage that you felt the need to drag it around all day?' He'd given her the key to his cabin—*their* cabin—right after they'd embarked a few hours ago. Wanting to give her some space to unpack, he'd found a quiet corner of the ship to go over his missed messages and emails. Most of them were from his parents, demanding answers he didn't have. Those remained unread.

'Well, funny you should ask. You see…' Catalina looked down to where her hand was clutching the white keycard. 'After I said goodbye to you—'

'After you stormed away while insulting my beard, yes.'

Colour rose to her cheeks, giving them an even softer glow. 'After I said goodbye and went to look for the cabin, I realised I didn't know which one was mine.'

Theo couldn't keep the smirk off his face. A few seconds ago he'd wanted nothing more than to get away from her before she could say anything else about his burnout and what her thoughts were on his utter failure as the head of emergency medicine at the hospital his parents had built from scratch. The one they'd expected to leave in his hands before he'd torched his life.

Something about Catalina—watching her stare at her hands in clear discomfort at having to ask *him* for a favour—cleared his head more than a meditative walk along the shoreline ever could. For a second, he forgot about the life events that had brought him here and could focus on the ease that was the antagonistic pattern he and Catalina had developed over the years.

'I see, so you've been wandering around the boat since earlier with your luggage, unsure where to put it. Why didn't you just call me?' Theo was pretty sure she didn't have his number, but details like that had never mattered to them when they sniped at each other.

His eyes dipped down to her lips when he noticed a muscle move in her jaw, enjoying the sight far more than he should. But focusing on that was better than trying to reconcile the changes in his life and where things would go after the cruise. Maybe that was why his sister had warned him to stay clear of her best friend. Catalina was already turning out to be an excellent distraction, and they'd spent no more than five minutes together.

'This is a ship, not a boat,' she said, and Theo couldn't help but laugh at the pure defiance in her voice. Not that it helped their situation as her glare turned angry.

'You've been part of the crew for a few hours and already an expert on all things boats—pardon, *ships*?'

Catalina let out a huff. 'A boat is smaller and can be controlled by an individual or a small team of people. A ship carries cargo or passengers and needs an entire crew to operate. Did you see how big the medical staff alone is here? Therefore, we are clearly on a ship.' Her sparkling brown eyes narrowed on him, and the sight affected him far more than it should. 'Did you do any research before coming here?'

Of course he had. From the moment he'd been born, he'd been trained by his parents to be the most type-A personality to ever walk the earth. But it was more fun to pretend otherwise.

'Not really. Amelie sent me some of the crap she'd researched, but it seemed frivolous.'

'Frivolous?' Catalina's voice pitch became higher, filling him with an inappropriate amount of glee.

He shrugged, playing at nonchalant. 'You know, things like "Top Ten Things to Do in Dubrovnik" or "Don't miss these three spots in Santorini". Not really helpful to life on a ship.'

'There was a lot more information in there outside of things to do in Santorini if you'd read it all carefully enough. Like a list of the most likely ailments we would encounter here, or what to do in case of an emergency.' Her speech sped up as she rattled off the information, and part of him wanted to let her know he'd read it all. And that he knew Catalina had been the one to put it all together. He knew his sister, and she had got all the spontaneity in the family.

'Is it buffets infested with norovirus?' he asked, recalling her previous comment.

'That's a big risk, believe it or not. But that's not why I followed you.' Her grip on her luggage tightened, tension flickering across her knuckles. 'Can you just show me the room?'

Right, the room they were supposed to share. There was no way that was going to happen, though Theo hadn't devoted much time to figuring out how to solve that particular problem. After dropping his stuff off, he'd needed a moment to regroup and make a plan of how the hell he was going to survive the next three weeks on this *ship*. One thing had become clear: there was no way they could share a room. Especially not *that* room.

He thought about telling her the glaring issue he'd encountered the moment he'd opened the door. But then he decided it would be funnier if she saw it with her own eyes.

'Fine, let's go,' he said, turning around and waving her along.

They weaved through different parts of the ship, taking the lift up with a group of people who had already hit the bar far harder than Theo would recommend this early in the afternoon. He looked at her over his shoulder when the lift stopped on the crew deck and felt her presence behind him as a prickle at the back of his neck.

The corridor buzzed with the thousand tiny operations that kept a ship like this from veering into chaos, despite feeling like chaos itself. Cabin doors clicked open and shut, voices scooted from room to room and the faint briny tang of the ocean soaked even the recycled air. Theo led them down two bends in the hall, then another, leading them into the bowels of the ship where the crew accommodation was.

He stopped in front of a nondescript door. The vinyl letters beside it read CREW DECK 8, CABIN 1264, and a tiny plastic placard below that read MORGAN/REYES, MD.

Theo let himself take a moment to appreciate the symmetry of their names, side by side like that. Only to quickly realise what he'd just done and push the thought away. They didn't live in a world where such a thought could move from fantasy to reality, and it was time he got a grip on it.

Not in the *before,* where he'd played too big a role in his family's legacy to let anyone get tangled up in the mess and misery that involved. And now, in the *after*, his life was a burning wreckage. In neither version had his attraction to his little sister's best friend ever made any sense.

It was unfortunate that now he faced three weeks of close proximity to her.

Theo tapped his keycard. 'After you.'

She entered and stopped dead. A laugh—almost a bark—escaped her. 'You have got to be kidding me.'

There it stood, just the way Theo remembered from when he'd arrived here a few hours ago: the single queen-sized bed jammed up against the far wall.

Catalina whirled around, eyes narrowed on him just as he entered. 'Did you do this?' she asked, and he couldn't swallow the incredulous snort.

'Yes, of course I planned this. When Amelie begged me to sub in for her so she wouldn't have to pay the contract termination fine, I thought to myself: You know what would make this whole thing even more *fun*? Sleeping in the same bed as my sister's best friend.'

She cut him a glare which, granted, he deserved for being a smartass. Something he needed to check himself over the next three weeks. Regressing to petty insults and jabs wasn't becoming of a doctor of his status. Even if doing so let him step away from the mess inside his head. As much as he wanted to, using Catalina to escape his own head was probably why Amelie had even felt the need to warn him about not doing anything 'inappropriate' with her best friend.

Stepping into the room, Catalina dropped her luggage on the rack with a *thunk* and then spun around once, inspecting the room. He watched her face as she twirled again, her eyes darting into every corner of the room. She frowned as she came to the same conclusion he'd reached when he had first come into the cabin.

'What about—'

'There's only a shower. No bathtub. Already checked. Not that I'd recommend either of us sleep in a bathtub for three weeks.' Theo had already made the decision to leave the room to Catalina and see if the ship had any open rooms. Even if he had to pay for his own room on the passenger side, he'd be happier than sleeping next to Catalina for the next three weeks. Not when he was already enjoying himself way too much in her presence.

Strange how a bit of needling could get him out of his head when nothing else had post-burnout.

'So…are we going to fight over it?' Catalina asked, her voice loud in the small space. 'Or is this one of those free-for-alls where we both pretend not to care and then one of us cracks and sleeps on the floor?'

'There isn't really much floor to go around,'

he replied, gesturing at their feet. Another thing he'd contemplated earlier and decided it wasn't a feasible option to solve this problem. But he was having too much fun watching her squirm to let her off the hook just yet. 'We could top and tail, strictly back-to-back. Minimal contact guaranteed.'

She rolled her eyes. 'Thank you for the helpful suggestion, Theodore. Clearly, you've never shared a double bed with three siblings before.' She crossed her arms and leaned against the desk, and Theo kept his eyes trained on her face even as he felt them draw downwards.

He forced a shrug, not admitting to either of them the effect her proximity had on him. 'No, I was busy being installed as the future of Western medicine. You know, the thing that sent me into...what did you call it? The *burnout thing*?'

Theo wasn't sure why he went there. What had led to his abrupt departure at Morgan Greywater was something he kept under lock and key. Amelie had tried multiple times to talk to him about it but he'd found he couldn't even mention what had happened. How he felt.

Now he stood here making jokes about the pressure under which he'd cracked, as if his decisions hadn't upended his life. This was not good.

Though his sister would argue that escape was something he desperately needed, it wasn't what he was looking for. But the relief of the pressure when he was near Catalina was already so seductive, he needed to stay away if he actually wanted to *work* through his issues during the cruise rather than drown himself in the next distraction.

Catalina didn't answer right away. For a moment, she just watched him, the teasing in her eyes dimmed to something quieter. Then, as if snapping herself out of it, she gave a shrug and turned to unzip her suitcase.

'Well, if you're planning on being insufferable, I call the right side.'

Theo snorted. 'I'll alert the media,' he said again because he couldn't help himself with her. He'd better leave now before she could drag him into something neither of them really wanted. 'I'll be back later. Need to talk some stuff through with Dr Chen.'

Theo didn't wait for her to look up from her packing, retracing his steps until he was back at the lifts. With each step, the knot in his chest that had eased during their entire conversation tightened again, reminding him of the work still in front of him. The cruise wasn't a chance to escape his life. No, he was doing it as a favour to his sister. Instead of getting distracted, he needed to spend his free time examining his life and figuring out where he was headed.

He had no job, no career, and his abrupt departure had left his reputation in tatters. After years of grinding, never-ending work, his professional contributions had been reduced to nothing. And he had no idea what he was supposed to do about that. If he had ever belonged in such a high-ranking position in the first place.

And yet, as he stepped into the lift and pressed the button to return to the reception area, his thoughts weren't on how to rebuild. They weren't on where he wanted to go with his life, either.

All he could think about was the smell of coconut butter on supple skin as he'd stood far too close to Catalina.

CHAPTER THREE

Day Four, at sea

THERE WERE FAR fewer opportunities to let her hair down than Catalina had anticipated. Yesterday they'd stopped in Kefalonia, but she had a shift at the clinic on that day and hadn't been able to leave the ship at all. Since then, they'd been at sea, crossing over the Ionian Sea on their way towards Corfu. Her heart had kicked up a beat standing on deck and watching the white stone walls appear. All her life, she hadn't even thought about going to Greece once. With a family as big as hers, their holidays had consisted of local adventures to different places in the Dominican Republic. Catalina hadn't set foot on a plane until her interview for med school in the United States.

Now she finally got to see the world. Sure, she got to see it in between treating mild cases of alcohol poisoning, the common cold and—surprisingly—an STI on her first day, but the point was, she was doing it. Seeing the world.

She was, however, not doing *it*. And with the situation she found herself in, she wasn't sure if project 'Cat loses her virginity' was still on. When she'd told Amelie she wanted to find someone to pop her cherry during the cruise, her best friend had squealed in excitement and promised she would vacate the room if she ever needed to bring her designated lover there.

Catalina wasn't sure Theo would extend the same courtesy. She certainly wasn't about to ask. Mainly because the only time she'd seen him had been in the clinic. Had he found somewhere else to sleep? He certainly hadn't come to the cabin at any point in the last four days; she would have noticed that. Still, what if he did come back the moment she asked someone to join her in bed?

The wind picked up as the ship approached the port. It tore at her clothes—a floral summer dress cinched tight at the waist and flaring out in a voluminous skirt—and a laugh slipped through her lips as Corfu's sun-washed villas and terracotta roofs gleamed against the hills thick with cypress and olive trees.

'Never seen anyone this excited to arrive at Corfu.' Theo's familiar drawl made her turn around and she watched him approach.

She hated how her breath hitched in her throat as her eyes roamed over him. Okay, yeah, he was a beautiful man. She avoided the word *handsome* because somehow it didn't seem enough.

He wasn't just intruding in the space of beautiful people, but he might actually have founded the club. Not that it mattered too much because his beauty didn't come with a kind personality. Quite the opposite.

'How many people have you seen arrive in Corfu in general?' she asked, crossing her arms in front of her to protect herself from his aura as well as to stop her hands from doing anything foolish like reaching out.

'That's fair enough. Let me rephrase: I don't think I've ever seen *you* this excited about anything.' He stepped next to her at the railing, leaning his hip against the metal bar, and looked out at the sea.

'Well, you haven't seen much of me since leaving med school.' She wasn't sure if the reminder was for him or for herself. Occasionally, Catalina had travelled back with Amelie to New York City, where the Morgan clan had built their empire, to celebrate Christmas and Thanksgiving. Amelie's family was plenty dysfunctional, but still miles ahead of the mess awaiting her back home in San Cristóbal. At least the Morgan parents had cared about their children's careers and pushed them towards excellence.

Whereas Catalina might as well not have bothered going to med school and becoming a doctor, her parents cared so little. Whenever she'd called them to tell them anything about her life—about her achievements—they had the same thing to say: *'That's nice, dear'*. Followed by whatever impressive thing Esteban, her oldest brother, had done. Like she gave a single crap that Esteban had added another van to the growing fleet of vehicles he rented out when she had helped to literally save someone's life on the same day.

Another problem Catalina had planned to deal with during her time on the cruise: her professional future. When starting her internship, she'd thought she would go into a specialty straight away. But the closer she'd got to the end, the less appealing the thought had become. But she *had* to continue her education, right? Pick a career path and excel at it, the way she always had.

What else could she do, if not the one thing she knew she was good at?

'The walls are so bright, it looks almost fake. More like a painting than real life,' he said, repeating her own thoughts from earlier almost verbatim, and ripping her out of her spiralling career crisis thoughts.

She shot him a sidelong glance, trying hard not to appreciate what she was seeing. Because he wasn't wearing what she would call typically Theo clothes. Even during the family holidays she'd spent at the Morgan estate, he'd worn what could only be described as business casual: a button-up shirt and chinos that were starched to oblivion and back. To the point where she'd been astounded about his ability to sit down. It was how he presented in front of patients in the clinic, too.

They'd worked together over the last few days, and the word *together* was doing a lot of heavy lifting. Occasionally they'd see each other as they popped their heads into the waiting room and asked people to come through. Unlike a structured GP clinic, their patients were all walk-ins, and they saw quite a few patients an hour. Which meant lots of bumping into each other.

Though today Theodore Morgan was wearing a loose white linen shirt and a pair of dark brown trousers of the same fabric and style. And Catalina couldn't swallow the surprised gasp when her eyes got all the way down to his feet.

'Are you wearing sandals?' The words shot out of her mouth before she could consider whether she even wanted to engage in more conversation with him. The answer was most likely no.

'Oh...yeah.' Theo looked down as well, as if he couldn't remember putting them on. 'Amelie gifted them to me.'

'I didn't take you as someone who'd wear sandals.'

'I don't. When my sister gave them to me, she said, "I've never seen you wear sandals so you must want some".' He chuckled, the sound low and strangely addictive. Catalina wouldn't mind hearing it again.

'That sounds just like her. You should see our

apartment in Chicago. It's filled to the brim with things she thought we could-slash-would use one day. Including a bread maker that's still in its original box.'

Something about their conversation was off, though Catalina couldn't figure out what it was. Maybe how easygoing it was? After sniping at each other the entire time on their first day, she'd thought the trend would continue whenever they saw each other. Except the only times they *had* seen each other had been at work. Which was odd, given…

'How come you haven't been back to our cabin?' she asked. She'd had the thought before but had put it off because a part of her didn't want to look beneath that rock if she didn't need to. Especially if this particular rock meant he might have found some other person he *didn't* mind sharing a bed with.

Catalina swatted the thought away so fast it had no time to sink its teeth into her.

'Oh? Miss me that much?' He smirked, running a hand through his short hair, the movement slow and deliberate.

She let out a sigh. 'Is this how it's going to be? Each time we see each other we either behave like children sniping at each other or like strangers?'

Theo turned to look at her, surprise rippling over his face. Had it never occurred to him they could be more than that? Not that Catalina had ever *really* considered it. Her little crush on him was mere physical attraction paired with annual forced proximity due to family visits. Her *interest*, if she could even call it that, had been one-sided from the start and was never meant to be acted on.

The thought alone was absurd.

A tremor ran through her when their eyes collided, a connection she'd been ignoring for years flaring back alive. He was the first to break eye contact as he dropped his head to stare down at the moving water beneath them. The silence stretched on, interrupted only by the passengers milling around them and the droning of the ship, which had already become so familiar she barely heard it.

Catalina was about to excuse herself and pretend she needed to get ready for the day in Corfu when Theo said, 'It's been nice handling the day-to-day in the clinic here. Less stressful. Almost feels like a vacation.'

He didn't raise his head as he spoke, and Catalina had to step closer to hear every word. There was an edge to his voice that drew her in. Could it be…vulnerability? Theo? No, that couldn't be right. In all the years she'd known him, he'd been stone-faced as a gargoyle in every single one of their interactions. To the point where Catalina had seriously questioned herself since she had developed a huge crush on this man that had hardly dulled in the years since he'd left med school.

'You prefer handling food poisoning over life-or-death situations in the ER?' she asked, though she knew the answer already. Had read studies about burnout in all disciplines of medicine, and those working with daily trauma were so much more likely to not just burnout but do irreversible damage to themselves.

A small smile curled his lips, though it didn't quite reach his eyes. 'Don't tell my parents. If they heard their son is enjoying the equivalent of family medicine, they'd probably send a team of doctors out to the cruise ship with sedatives and a straitjacket.'

Theo was passing it off as a joke, but she suspected there was more behind his words. She and Amelie shared everything with each other. Everything except things about Theo. Catalina had never questioned it because the less she knew about him—the less she was *around* him—the sooner this pesky infatuation would go away. The crush itself was too clichéd for her to stand it. The young impressionable med student from a poor upbringing falls for the protege of a prestigious medical dynasty? *Gag.* She'd seen that plot unravel in several medical TV dramas.

Whether Amelie was protective of her brother or she was looking out for Catalina and her dumb crush, she didn't know. She wasn't even sure if Amelie had ever suspected what fuelled the antagonism between Catalina and Theo. No matter if she did or didn't, her best friend never talked about her brother or what was happening in his life.

But Catalina wasn't blind. She knew when a person was struggling. And that wasn't something she could walk away from.

Swallowing the sigh—and the roiling in her stomach warning her that spending any extra time with Theo would be a bad idea—Catalina straightened up and asked, 'Seeing how you're dressed, you're going to see Corfu today?'

The question made him look up, and the intensity in his eyes was as sudden as it was brief. Then his usual gargoyle expression fell back into place. 'Thought I might have a walk around since I didn't get to leave the boat in Kefalonia.'

'Yeah, me neither.' She paused, unsure how to approach this. Maybe she was misreading this entire situation and he wasn't lonely. He didn't need her help with anything. 'Do you want to see the island together? Fair warning, the detailed itinerary Amelie shared with you was mine and I intend on hitting every single spot at the intended time.'

His brows shot up, and she wished the stony expression back. Because the look rippling across his face right now did something annoying to her stomach. Made it swoop like she'd boarded a roller coaster. 'I should have figured my sister didn't write this.'

'Oh, yeah? How come?'

Wrong question because it made his lips kick up in a smile—a genuine one this time that reached his eyes in a sparkle.

'Because Amelie hasn't organised anything in her entire life. I'm surprised she even made it through med school.'

Catalina laughed, the knot in her chest loosening a fraction. 'I think we pulled each other through it. Me by sharing all of my notes with her, while she reminded us to take breaks, hydrate and eat normal food and not just instant noodles.'

Though even to this day nothing hit quite as right as some instant noodles blasted in the microwave.

'I don't think anyone has ever survived med school without copious amounts of microwavable noodles,' he said, earning himself another laugh.

'Literally what I was thinking right now!'

The wind picked up, tearing at their clothes, and around them some passengers gave excited squeals as the port manifested in front of them.

Crew hurried around, yelling things into their walkie-talkies, and Catalina thought the entire thing might have been overwhelming. Except there was one person she was focused on, with the bustling of the ship no more than irritating background noise.

Was he really going to make her ask again?

'So…?' This was as far as she would go. The ball was in his court. If she had to repeat herself, she would shift from casual to needy, and that was not something she would do with Theodore.

He straightened, towering over her enough that she had to stare up at him. The wind tousled his hair, sending the strands in a myriad of directions. It was longer than it had been when she'd last seen him for his father's seventieth birthday party. He'd kept it cropped ever since he'd started in the ER at Morgan Greywater, not letting it get any longer than a centimetre. The last time she'd seen it this long had been during their shared year at med school, and back then she'd already wondered far too often what it would be like to feel the silky strands between her fingers.

Oops. Nope, not where her thoughts should be going. Damn it.

'Sure, let's go,' he said, yanking her out of her thoughts.

'Wait, really?' Even though she'd asked the question, Catalina hadn't expected a positive reply. Since when did Theodore Morgan hang out with anyone?

But this wasn't the man she knew. This was the *after* version of whatever had happened to him in that ER. He was almost the same. *Almost*. Except she'd seen the cracks during this conversation without anyone needing to mention them or point towards them. Hell, that he was even here instead of continuing his legacy at Morgan

Greywater was a testament to how much trouble he really was in.

Theo shrugged, either because she'd read too much into it or because he wanted to play this moment of vulnerability down. Did it matter? 'You seem to have a plan, and I've not thought through anything other than stretching my legs. So why not?'

When she'd issued the invitation, Catalina hadn't expected him to accept. Leaving her now to puzzle over the appropriate response here.

'Okay, then…but keep up with me. If we want to see anything, there is no margin for lingering and *enjoying the scenery*.'

The flash of teeth accompanying his grin shot right down her spine, and before she could react outwardly, she took a step back and clutched her phone with the itinerary mapped out.

This was fine. Theo was clearly going through some stuff and she was being a good person. A good best friend, looking after Amelie's broken brother.

Totally fine.

CHAPTER FOUR

Day Four, Corfu

THIS DIDN'T COUNT as getting closer, right? The thought ate at Theo as they walked up one of the winding streets of Corfu.

They'd started their day weaving through the cobbled alleyways of Corfu Town, the smell of strong coffee and orange blossom clinging to the warm morning air. Bright shutters lined the pastel buildings, most cracked open to let in the breeze. They'd passed a sleepy *kafeneio* where two old men were deep in a game of *tavli*, dice clicking against the wooden board, arguing in murmurs that sounded affectionate even in disagreement.

Later, they'd wandered up to the Old Fortress, its weathered stone walls casting long shadows as the sun climbed higher. Catalina had insisted on taking the narrow steps up to the top, where the view had stunned even Theo into silence—an endless blue horizon broken by the curve of the coastline, the rooftops below tiled in sun-warmed terracotta.

Now, hours later, their route had grown quieter. The cruise tourists had thinned, replaced by sun-struck cats and the distant echo of a church bell. Wrought-iron balconies overflowed with bougainvillea and drying laundry, and the scent of grilled sardines drifted from a tiny taverna with checked tablecloths and no English menu.

No, this definitely didn't count. If anything, Amelie would be thrilled he'd left the ship behind for the day. Wasn't that why she'd sent him Catalina's itinerary in the first place? So he could find some inspiration and get out there? Except what he couldn't figure out was why she hadn't altered it. Wouldn't she have figured out that if he followed the same itinerary as Catalina, they would bump into each other? It flew in the face of his sister's request to stay away from her best friend.

So did the room situation. To his utter bafflement, there had been no open rooms on the ship according to the reception desk, leaving him with no alternative than to sleep on one of the stretchers in the clinic. Thankfully, Dr Chen seemed to assume he was just resting rather than squatting, and he had yet to explain himself to anyone.

And until a few hours ago, Catalina hadn't even seemed to notice his absence. When she'd asked, he'd wanted to tell her the truth. He'd decided to find somewhere else to stay for her comfort. He was only one step above a stranger, and there was no scenario in which he was comfortable forcing his presence on someone like that.

'Have you ever been to Greece before?' Catalina asked in between breaths. The island was deceptively hilly, each new destination forcing them up and down several hills to the point of exhaustion.

He shook his head. 'I haven't spent any time travelling that wasn't for work. And most of that was fairly local. Medical conferences and such. Close enough to get back to New York City if required.'

It sounded just as pathetic out loud as in his head. He'd built his entire life around this one job—the legacy he'd never asked for—and had given up so much of his life, only to lose it all in the span of a week.

Less than that. When he'd reached his limit, he'd simply got up from his desk and walked out, not thinking about the consequences. Those had come later and were still plaguing him now.

'Me neither. It's my first time in Europe,' she said, keeping the conversation on the light side of things—just as she had since they'd disembarked. 'Whatever free time I had during med school I spent studying, like the try-hard I am. The only place I'd ever travel to was back home.'

They had this much in common: giving far too much of themselves to the pursuit of greatness.

Though he looked for the signs he'd ignored in himself in Catalina, and he couldn't see any of them. Maybe it was the reason she was here, seeing what had happened to him. How he'd only stepped back when it had been already too late.

'Home is the Dominican Republic for you, yes?' Theo framed it as a question even though he knew the answer. There wasn't a single thing he'd learned about Catalina Reyes he had forgotten over the years of knowing her.

She nodded, her smile more subdued than it had been a moment ago. 'It's what we're told to call it. *Home*. Regardless of how accurate it feels.'

They reached another taverna with its seats spilling out onto the cobbles. The menu sat on a stand right outside the door and when Catalina approached it, she clapped her hands in excitement. 'Never thought I'd be this happy to see the Latin alphabet.' Before Theo could ask what she meant with that comment about home, she whirled around with a smile bright enough to blind him. 'Let's have a bite to eat.'

'Does that even fit in today's agenda? I would have thought you'd make us eat sandwiches while walking.' He actually didn't mind that idea, but Theo wasn't about to tell her that her tour of Corfu had been so much better than he could have imagined. He might go as far as to say he was enjoying himself.

Not something he'd done in the recent past.

'Please, you think I'd plan a visit to a Greek isle and not plan a stop for real Greek food? How foolish do you think I am?' She shook her head, and when he nodded his agreement she plopped herself down on a chair with him taking the one opposite.

When the waiter approached them, Catalina leaned forward with a smile that could charm stone. 'Hi! Can we get—' She paused and tilted her head. 'What's your most traditional dish that doesn't involve lamb? I'm trying not to eat mammals today. I had a moment with a goat statue earlier and now I'm emotionally compromised.'

The waiter, perhaps used to odd tourist declarations, only smiled. 'Moussaka without meat? Or perhaps spanakopita, dolmades, grilled halloumi?'

'That,' she said, pointing to the halloumi, wide-eyed and licking her lips. 'And the dolmades. And tzatziki. And—Theo, what are you having?'

'I'm being guided by a woman who fell in love with a goat statue, so clearly I'll trust your judgement,' he said, then turned to the waiter. 'Same for me. And maybe a Greek salad for the table?'

Catalina gave a little approving nod, as if he'd passed a test. Why did that send a thrill down his spine?

'Good choice. You're learning.'

Their water came first, ice cubes clinking in mismatched glasses. For a few minutes they drank in silence that was more companionable than strained, the quiet broken only by the hum of traffic a few streets down and the clatter of plates from inside the taverna. Theo let himself lean back into the metal chair and—just briefly—breathe.

This was almost peaceful, each lungful of air filling him with the tranquillity of the island. Muscles which had been bunched up from the moment he'd left med school relaxed, knots loosening, and for a moment he let himself believe that life might be this simple after all. That the consequences that awaited him back home didn't matter. That he didn't torch his family's entire legacy by leaving the hospital one evening and never returning.

The legacy that had been slowly killing him day by day.

'See? I told you.' Catalina's voice drifted across the table, warm and teasing. 'I know where the good stuff is.'

'Not the worst place you've brought me,' he admitted, unable to keep the smile from his face.

Her eyes brightened, flicking over him. 'Considering I've never brought you anywhere, I don't think this is the compliment you pretend it is. Unless this is you inviting yourself along to any other stops when we both have the day off.'

Theo realised he didn't hate the idea. His original plan had entailed nothing more than doing his sister a favour. He'd not thought about what else there would be to do outside of his shifts. But a calm he hadn't felt in far too long infused him, and so the next words came out without much resistance.

'If you'll have me.'

Catalina's lips parted, still wet from the water she'd drunk. For a second, she looked as if she was going to say something, but the waiter reappeared with their food, a riot of colour and comfort across the tabletop. The halloumi was crispy and golden, tasting like light and salt and grease. They stabbed into each other's plates with mismatched forks, trading and tasting and pushing the salad back and forth between them.

'Here.' Catalina's eyes were intent, watching for his reaction as she held out a vine leaf wrapped tight around fragrant rice. Her fingers brushed his, and he took it from her hand, his own hand clumsy and too slow. When he bit in, she cocked her head, appraising his expression. 'Well?'

'Not bad,' he said, wiping oil from his mouth. 'But I still prefer sandwiches on the go.'

She clicked her tongue. 'I knew Amelie was uncultured, but I didn't realise this applied to you, too. Didn't you attend all sorts of fancy galas and fundraisers as the heir apparent of the Morgan family?'

Theo's entire body stiffened at her words, the warmth that had just begun to settle in fleeing on the breeze brushing over them. Even though it was nothing more than polite conversation and something anyone could ask, it was a reminder of everything waiting back home. Everything he didn't know how to deal with yet.

She must have caught the shift in his expression because she went wide-eyed and said, 'Sorry, what I meant to say was—'

'It's fine,' he said too quickly, trying to look casual as he stabbed his fork into the salad. 'You're right. I did a lot of those things. Not that I had much of a choice. I had to be there.'

Was it too much to admit that to Catalina? Compared to everything else he was keeping locked away, it was the smallest of truths. But it still left him feeling exposed, like an unhealed scrape.

Catalina fell silent, the kind of heavy silence that seemed to unspool between breaths until she eventually said, 'I grew up thinking that families like yours must be perfect. That it must be so easy to have parents who care about your life and want you to succeed. But even though Amelie dances to her own tune, she told me how hard it had been to defy her parents' expectations of her. And how they all fall on you now. It's so unlike my family, who...'

She didn't finish, but he knew what came next. That the grass wasn't greener, and that his story wasn't much different from hers. Always reaching. Never good enough.

'Living someone else's dream is never easy, is it?'

Understanding bloomed on her face and it hit him in a way he hadn't expected. It showed him that even though this woman had spent a fair amount of time at his family's home, he didn't know all that much about her. Didn't know her circumstances, her upbringing or what lay beneath the beautiful façade.

Catalina opened her mouth, brows drawing together as if she was choosing her words with care.

A sharp crash broke through the haze of their conversation. At the far end of the taverna's patio, a chair scraped against stone. A man had slumped sideways, limbs limp, a knocked-over glass of wine seeping into the tablecloth. His dining partner—a woman with cropped grey hair—was already shouting, voice rising in panic.

'James? James!'

Theo was out of his chair before she'd even finished saying his name.

The other diners froze, forks halfway to mouths. Catalina's chair screeched against the stone as she stood, moving to follow. Her expression had dropped all trace of humour, hands steady even as adrenaline surged behind her eyes.

Theo crouched beside the man, pressing fingers to his carotid. 'Pulse is faint,' he said aloud for Catalina's benefit, and maybe his own.

The man's skin was clammy, his face rapidly draining of colour. His breathing was shallow, lips tinged a bluish-grey.

'Sir? Can you hear me?' Theo asked, shaking his shoulder gently. No response.

'Could be a syncopal episode,' Catalina murmured, already pulling her phone from her bag. 'Or hypoglycaemia?'

Theo shook his head once. 'Call emergency services. If we can stabilise him, we'll let the local team handle transport.'

She nodded and stepped away, already dialling. Theo caught the clipped edge of English as she spoke into the phone, slow and clear, pausing when the operator asked something she clearly didn't understand. 'Corfu Town, yes. A tourist collapsed at a restaurant. We need medical help.' She looked around, locking eyes with Theo first and then the waiter, who hurried over to her as she put emergency services on speakerphone.

Knowing Catalina had it covered, he turned back to the patient on the floor. 'Breathing's becoming more shallow,' he muttered, then raised his voice. 'Ma'am? Does he have any medical conditions? Medications?'

The woman was frozen, her hands fluttering at her chest. 'I think it's his blood sugar,' she said, breath hitching. 'He's type two diabetic—but he's on insulin. I know most people aren't, but he's had it for years, and it just got worse. The tablets weren't enough any more, and the consultant said his pancreas was basically giving up. But James, h-he watches what he eats and everything…but this morning…this morning he skipped breakfast because we were late, and I told him it was a bad idea, but he said he felt fine—'

She stopped when Catalina put a hand on her shoulder, giving it a squeeze. Her tone was soft when she said, 'He may have taken insulin without food to buffer it. Thank you for telling us. We'll help him, okay?' The woman's panicked eyes searched Catalina's face and then, trusting, let her hands drop.

'Theo,' she said when she crouched down next to him. 'Ambulance is en route, but they didn't give an ETA. Could be a while.'

He nodded, gaze sweeping over the patient again. 'We need glucose. Do you know whether he has anything with him?'

The woman blinked, as if trying to shake herself out of a fog. 'His bag—he has a little pouch, but I don't know what he keeps in there. He doesn't like it when I get involved in his medical stuff.'

'Check it,' Theo said, then turned to the waiter who was hovering nearby, eyes wide. 'Do you have juice? Coke? Anything with sugar?'

The waiter nodded and bolted back into the taverna.

Catalina reappeared at Theo's side a beat later, already crouching with the pouch in hand. 'Insulin pens, glucometer, but no snacks.' She flicked it open, reading the monitor's last log. 'Last reading was five point nine mmol/L but that was yesterday.'

Theo swore under his breath. 'We'll have to assume he's hypoglycaemic. If we can get sugar into him orally and he's conscious enough to swallow, we'll do that. Otherwise, we're going to have to find another way.'

The waiter returned with a glass of orange juice sloshing wildly in his hand. 'Is this okay?'

'It'll work,' Theo said. He turned to the patient prone on the floor again. 'James? Can you hear me?' Still no response.

Catalina leaned closer, voice low and even. 'His eyes are fluttering. I think he's semi-conscious.' She tapped his cheek gently. 'James, you with us?'

There was a faint groan.

'That's something,' Theo muttered. 'Let's try.'

With Catalina supporting the patient's head, Theo tipped a bit of the juice into his mouth. The man coughed and choked, but then swallowed. Theo glanced at Catalina, who nodded once.

'Keep going. Small sips.'

A small crowd had begun to gather now, tourists peering over from their tables, some filming, others whispering. The air had grown tight with tension, the late afternoon heat suddenly oppressive.

'We need space,' Catalina called out, her voice calm but firm. 'Please give us some room.'

The woman—James's partner—looked up. 'Is he going to be okay? He was fine this morning. I don't understand.'

Catalina put on a soft smile again, and Theo fought not to get distracted by it. There were too many things jumping at him right now and vying for his attention. Like the way her hands cradled their patient's head with such care. How she kept James's frantic loved one updated even as she helped Theo handle this situation.

It made him realise how little he really knew about her. He didn't know what kind of doctor she was, how she dealt with the pressure of the job, or even how she preferred to practise medicine. What was she going to do once the cruise was over? Travel medicine? Or a less adventurous specialism? Whatever it would be, he knew her ambition was boundless.

He pushed those thoughts away when the patient on the floor stirred. Minutes passed in tense silence, broken only by the clink of the glass as Theo coaxed another sip past James's lips. Then—slowly—colour returned to the man's face. He blinked, eyes glassy but open. 'Lynne…?'

The woman gasped, crouching beside them. ‘I’m here, love. I’m right here.’

James’s hand moved, seeking hers, and Theo let out a breath. ‘He’s coming back.’

Catalina pulled back at the same time, her shoulder brushing Theo’s. ‘We stabilised him.’

He nodded, still scanning James for any sign of relapse, but the worst seemed to have passed.

Sirens echoed faintly in the distance.

Catalina looked at him. ‘You did well.’

‘So did you,’ he said. And for a moment—surrounded by the mess of knocked-over chairs, sweat on his brow and adrenaline in his blood—he felt something more than just relief. He’d expected a familiar pressure to push on his chest, the crushing sensation of an incoming anxiety attack unfurling in the pit of his stomach. It was how he’d felt every time he’d set foot in the ER of Morgan Greywater the last few months before he’d quit.

But the emergency had triggered none of that. His adrenaline had spiked, of course it had, but then he’d jumped into action and…

Theo looked up at Catalina, who sent him a tentative smile. As far as emergencies went, this wasn’t even comparable to what he used to handle, but something about the situation—them working together—struck him.

Support. Throughout this entire emergency, Catalina had done everything he needed for support without even asking. Why was that a novel experience? Had it been something lacking at Morgan Greywater? He remembered his colleagues with fondness, the team trying their hardest in any situation. The pressure hadn't come from a lack of support, but rather the expectations piling on top of him, and each time he'd fallen short he'd not only let his family down but everyone he was in charge of, too.

The sirens grew louder, and the ambient chatter of the taverna fell as the ambulance jerked to a halt nearby. A pair of paramedics rushed over and they transferred James to a stretcher. He was already more alert.

Lynne hovered beside him, her expression a mixture of gratitude and lingering panic. 'Thank you,' she said, and took Catalina's hand. 'You saved his life.'

'You did,' Catalina replied, squeezing back. 'You told us everything we needed to know.'

Theo watched the exchange, a small smile tugging at the corner of his mouth. Watching Catalina work was…surprising. Impressive.

Goddamn irresistible.

With the patient en route to the hospital and the crowd dispersing, they found themselves alone amid the debris of their meal.

The adrenaline should've worn off by now, but Theo felt charged, as if every nerve-ending was awake and alive. He glanced at Catalina even though he knew he shouldn't. It would only give the *thing* inside him room to breathe.

Hadn't he promised his sister he'd stay away from Catalina? Theo had made the promise without thinking, because of course he wouldn't start anything with Catalina. The thought had never crossed his mind.

Now that he was in her orbit, he remembered what she was like. The magnetism humming between them whenever they clashed. How much fun it was to have verbal sparring matches with her.

How Catalina marched to the beat of her own drum, always making him wish he could do that, too. And wasn't he doing it now?

'Most exciting meal I've had in a while,' he said, and she let out a shaky laugh.

'I thought you were going to say fastest. Did we even get to that salad?'

'I think we inhaled most of it,' he replied, letting the familiar back-and-forth ground him. The aforementioned salad had, of course, gone mostly untouched between all the other delicacies they'd ordered. But they'd reached a silent understanding: they would both pretend to have thoroughly enjoyed it. They were doctors, after all.

'Thanks for your quick reaction,' he said when silence settled between them, and Catalina waved her hand.

'It's kind of why we got hired in the first place,

right?' The corner of her mouth kicked up, and he felt himself return the smile before he could think otherwise.

'I guess. Though this might count as overtime. We should ask Dr Chen about that.' Around them, tourists were flooding the streets, most of them heading back in the direction of the port.

'Wait, doctors get overtime?' Catalina widened her eyes in what he knew to be mock shock. 'How could Morgan Greywater even afford to spend all of that extra money?'

The mention of his family's hospital was like a bucket of ice water decanted directly into his veins. His muscles seized, his body reverting to the same fight-or-flight reaction that had pushed him through endless days and nights in the emergency room, trying to hold all of it together through sheer will. So much time and effort given of himself, so many opportunities to lead a normal life passed over, only for him to lose it all. To give it away.

Cracked under the pressure of his last name.

The shock on Catalina's face turned genuine as she no doubt read his body language. Not for the first time, he wondered how much Amelie had told her about him. It couldn't be all that much considering he'd kept most of the things haunting him internal. His sister had broken through the toxic cycle of the obligations that came with their family name, and he didn't plan on dragging her back into it by telling her what had happened to him.

'I think we need to get back to the boat. Dr Chen won't be happy if they leave without us,' he said, both to move on from the topic and to have an excuse to turn away from her as they threaded into the flow of people around them heading in the same direction.

CHAPTER FIVE

Day Five, at sea

OKAY, SO THEODORE MORGAN wasn't *only* a foul-tempered man with a hot face and an even hotter body. Underneath the stony façade lurked a surprisingly funny guy. Or maybe she was just telling herself that. Maybe she was chickening out on starting her new life by hanging out with him rather than focusing on the pleasure that—theoretically—awaited her on the social side of the boat. Even on her days off, she'd not set foot in any of the seven bars or three nightclubs *The Aurelian* offered its guests. At least not until today, when she'd sat down with a drink at an empty table and had begun staring at the crowd, as if she could find a suitable mate like that.

It was the most effort Catalina could muster right now. She'd told herself it was because of the unresolved Theo situation. How was she supposed to bring someone over if Theo could pop into their room at any second? She was already nervous enough about finding a hot stranger and getting rid of her virginity. Maybe thinking of it as 'getting rid of it' was part of the problem. But with almost a week of the cruise and no sign of him ever sleeping in their shared accommodation, she kind of knew he'd found some other place to stay.

There were no traces of him after all. No luggage with his clothes. No toothbrush in their shared bathroom. And she had yet to wake up in the middle of the night with him sleeping on the floor like some homeless raccoon.

Wait, weren't raccoons homeless by default? The thought made her laugh out loud, and a few heads turned towards her. Fair enough. She'd also be glancing at the lonely lady laughing by herself in the corner of the room with an untouched drink sitting right in front of her.

The truth was simple: Catalina had no idea how to pick up anyone. It was the reason she was still a virgin at the delicate age of twenty-six. Between vying for her parents' attention by outperforming at literally everything she had tackled—and never getting the praise she craved—and then throwing herself into the most competitive and high-performing medical program in the country, she'd had no time or energy to figure out dating. She'd made exactly one friend—Amelie—and had nailed it on the first try.

To Catalina's dismay, she'd also only ever developed one crush—Theodore—and a part of her blamed his sheer proximity more than anything else. Was his lush dark hair the envy of every man crossing his path? Probably. Did his gaze send tingles running up and down her spine? Unfortunately. Was he going to be the one to take her virginity? Not a chance in hell. He wouldn't give her the time of day even if her life depended on it.

Except he had taken her up on the offer to explore Corfu Town together, and hadn't it been sort of nice? Not date-nice, and definitely not 'let me make sweet love to you' nice. But…like… friendly? Comfortable? When their conversation had veered into more personal space, she'd thought she had glimpsed something beneath the stony exterior. Another soul fighting a battle for parental appreciation, even if it came in a completely different shape.

Ugh, feeling a sympathetic spark for Theodore Morgan was the opposite of what Catalina needed right now. Sure, they had fun on Corfu, and maybe he wasn't as stern and gargoyle-y as she'd always thought. But still, what was one nice day compared to all the times she'd met him and he hadn't even found her worthy of his attention?

'You look like you could use some company.'

Catalina yanked her head up from where she'd been inspecting the table in all of its magnificence and stared into the unfamiliar face of…some guy? Maybe a patient?

She tried to place him since he was looking at

her rather expectantly. Had they spoken on her last shift?

And then it clicked. Her lips parted as she let out an 'oh' sound. Her spine stiffened the moment she realised he wasn't here to see her in her professional capacity. He was here because he'd seen a woman sitting by herself at a table at a bar, and he was trying his luck.

This was the moment she'd been waiting for. Someone was hitting on her. Only whenever she'd gone through the scenario in her head there had been no doubt about it, unlike right now. And her first reaction to the person hitting on her hadn't been mild confusion followed by instant discomfort.

'I'm not *not* looking for company,' Catalina said, cringing right away. She should have really taken some flirting lessons ahead of this trip. Was that even a thing? It sounded bizarre, but surely capitalism would find a way.

'May I?' The guy stared at the empty chair next to her, and she forced herself to nod. Truth be told she didn't want to spend any time with this stranger, but the idea flew in the face of the whole 'losing your virginity in a fun night of debauchery' idea so she really had to accept when the universe threw opportunities her way.

A picture of Theo flashed through her mind, and she pushed it away before any dumb ideas could take root. His being here and sharing a cabin with her, at least in theory, was *not* the universe's way of getting her to take a hint.

Nope.

'I'm Dave,' the guy said, holding out his hand towards her.

Okay, Dave. Unorthodox move, starting with a handshake, but Catalina needed to keep an open mind. Maybe handshakes were popular again. Or an essential part of the dating experience. With her having done exactly zero dating, she needed to take the lead from other people.

A shiver ran down her spine when his fingers wrapped around her hand with far too little pressure, leaving a clammy imprint behind. She fought with all the strength inside her to keep her expression neutral. This flirting business wasn't off to a good start.

'I'm Cat,' she replied, dropping her hand down into her lap and hoping he didn't notice her gently wiping it on her thigh.

Definitely not a good start.

'Oh, Cat. I like it.' His face split into a far too eager grin as he made a cat noise and bent his fingers so they looked like claws. 'Why is a cute kitten like you sitting all by yourself at the edge of the party? I almost didn't see you.'

He made a sweeping motion behind him. The bass of the electronic music was strong enough to rattle the furniture the closer it was to the source. Catalina had spent two minutes in there before finding this table and making it her home for the evening. How could she even approach anyone when it required screaming through a conversation?

And had this guy really just called her a cute kitten? Instant boner killer. Or whatever one said for the female version. Dry peach?

'It's a bit too loud in there. I was giving my ears a break,' she said, attempting a smile that said, *I'm not all that interested in talking to you.* It clearly didn't work, since Dave kept staring at her with that smile on his face.

'Right, right. Not so easy to chat someone up. I thought so too.' The way he nodded had her believing he hadn't thought about it for even a second.

Dave leaned in, his arm brushing against hers on the table, and gave her a once-over that wasn't even pretending to be discreet. 'So, are you one of the dancers or something? You've got that look.'

Catalina blinked. 'The…look?'

'Yeah. You've got this sexy, mysterious vibe. Bet you're trouble.'

He winked, and it took everything in her not to recoil. She reached for her drink just to have something to do, fingers curling tightly around the glass.

'Not really. I'm a doctor working at the clinic here. So I'm part of the crew and not a regular guest.' This interaction was turning into a mistake. Nothing about Dave was giving her the reaction she knew would be essential to take him back to her room—or, rather, ask him to take her to his. Inexperienced as she was, she knew the amount of cringe running through her body as he looked at her wasn't the way to go.

Nothing about this felt like a spark. No flutter in her stomach, no tilt in the world, no inexplicable rush of heat that made her catch her breath. None of the things that—annoyingly—had started to happen around Theo.

Like when he'd brushed past her in that tiny exam room, close enough that her pulse had jumped without permission. Or when he'd made some grumpy offhand comment, and she'd found herself smiling at the crinkle in his brow instead of the words.

God, was her body *actually* so broken that it only responded to sarcasm and disapproval in a six-foot-something grump?

'A sexy doctor. That's even better,' Dave drawled, hinting at his inebriated state, and Catalina took that as her sign to extract herself from this table, call it a night and try again the next day. Practice made perfect and all that. She offered a tight-lipped smile and angled her body away ever so slightly. He either didn't notice or didn't care.

'I've always had a thing for women who take

charge. You're the kind of girl who likes to be in control, huh?' He grinned, as if it was a compliment.

All right, time to go, she told herself as she set her glass down. Bracing her hands on the table, she said, 'Sorry, but I should—'

'Hey, don't go yet. I'm not done talking to you.' His hand landed on her arm. Light. Casual. But enough to snap a warning into her system.

Forced to lean closer, she could smell the alcohol on his breath and it sent another shiver through her. Her eyes narrowed, and she flexed her hand, ready to give this guy what he was asking for by laying a hand on her.

'You've clearly had too much to drink to have a pleasant conversation with anyone. I suggest you go sleep it off,' she said, but when she pulled her hand free of his grip she saw it darting straight back at her.

She flinched instinctively, but instead of touching her again, his hand stilled in mid-air. Stopped there, to be precise, by another hand wrapping around his wrist with a grip hard enough that Dave yelped.

So did Catalina when she followed the muscular arm up and found the rest of Theo staring at the guy accosting her. His eyes had a dangerous spark in them as he stared the drunk guy down. Nothing in his stony expression let her glimpse what he might be thinking.

Not until he spoke, voice low and rumbling. 'I believe she said she's not interested,' he said, every word somehow also a threat.

'She did not. I'd never bother someone who said no.' Dave wiggled his hand, but Theo's grip didn't falter, turning tight enough that she could see his knuckles whitening.

'A hint for next time: when someone gets up to make an exit, it means they don't want to be there. So don't go grabbing them to restrain them,' Theo said, and why were his words sparking something low in her stomach?

Dave blinked, first at her and then up at Theo. 'Oh, mate, I didn't realise she was with you. Totally my bad. I didn't mean anything by it.'

Theo simply stared at him, a muscle in his jaw jumping for a few quiet seconds before he let go of the guy's hand. 'I'd better not see you anywhere near her again. *Mate*.'

The guy vanished as fast as he had appeared, leaving Catalina alone with Theo's brooding presence and the unfortunate conundrum where she found herself indebted to him. The least she could do was thank him, even if the thought sent nervous flutters through her.

'You don't have to thank me,' he said, seemingly reading her mind. Was her anguish that obvious, or was it possible that Theo actually knew her?

'Of course I have to. You helped me out of a

potentially sticky situation. I would be a bit of an ass not to acknowledge that at the very least,' she replied, and debated for a second if that was enough of a thank you, before sadly coming to the conclusion that it was not.

Plopping down on the chair she'd just got up from, she let out a sigh and gestured at the other chair for Theo to sit. He did after a moment of hesitation. The low drumming of the bass filled the space between them, and Catalina reached out to run her fingers up and down her empty glass, just to give her hands something to do.

Intellectually, she knew what was about to happen. Dave's unwanted attention had triggered a spike in adrenaline, making her ready to fight. Now that the issue was resolved, the adrenaline was coming back down, and with it came the familiar symptoms of the crash: shaky limbs, shallow breathing and a ridiculous awareness of how tight her dress suddenly felt against her chest. Textbook catecholamine dump.

Fight-or-flight, now firmly in the post-game analysis phase.

She'd read about it. She'd lectured patients about it. But somehow, knowing what her autonomic nervous system was doing in clinical terms didn't stop her from feeling the lingering heat on her skin or the way her pulse kept fluttering as if it hadn't quite decided whether it was still in danger.

Which was absurd. The threat was gone. Theo was here. And that was *not* a soothing thought.

If anything, he'd made it worse by showing up like some dark knight with a grudge against unsolicited touching. And now he was sitting across from her, looking at her as if he wasn't sure whether to ask if she was okay or interrogate her about her poor decision-making.

She hated how steady he looked. How composed.

As if *he* hadn't just gone from zero to dangerous in five seconds flat.

'Did Amelie tell you why she was dragging me to this cruise?' she asked to take her mind off the riot of sensations pouring through her body. Catalina was almost certain she would regret opening up, but right now she needed to say anything to keep her mind off the dampness of her sweat clinging to her.

Theo leaned back in his chair, his eyes fixed on the window to their side and watching the dark sky pass them by. 'Just assume my sister has told me absolutely nothing about anything. Ever. And even then you'd assume too much,' he said, and it was enough to make her look up.

'What? I know you guys are close. She texts you all the time.'

Truly, it was hard to tell her best friend *not* to share things.

Theo let out a low chuckle, which somehow

crossed the space between them and slithered down her spine in a pleasant spark of warmth. 'She sends me anywhere between seven and twenty-four Instagram reels a day, and that's about it. Her style of communication when it comes to me is very much "interpretive memes".'

Catalina let out a laugh, because she couldn't have described Amelie any better. 'You should see the artwork she's put up in our apartment.'

'Oh, I'm well aware of Shrek adorning the wall above the fireplace. Unclear if the artist painted this erotic rendition of Shrek under duress.' His lips twitched in what Catalina knew to be his version of a smile. Theo leaned forward, bracing his arms on the table, and his gaze swept over her. 'You okay?'

'Yeah, of course I am.' She said it reflexively and cringed when the hollowness of her voice reached her ears. It wasn't lost on Theo, either. His lips pulled into a frown and his gaze swept over her, scrutinising. The hair along her arms stood on end at the intensity in his eyes.

'Catalina.' It was all he said. Yet hearing her name in his dark voice cracked something inside her. Maybe it was the disappointment this week had been so far regarding her mission of finally getting with someone. Or that she was all alone on this ship when she was supposed to have her best friend by her side. Or maybe it was this thing between her and Theo, the elusive push and pull that had existed since they'd met all those years ago—now exacerbated by their forced proximity to one another.

Though how forced was it at this point? Catalina would never admit it even under oath, but the day out in Corfu had been far better than she'd expected. Sure, wandering around with Theo had put a considerable dampener on any conversation she might have had with any eligible bachelor. Or bachelorette. Or non-binary babe.

With her lack of experience, Catalina wasn't fussy. The point of this cruise had been to explore her sexuality at warp speed as she approached her thirties, since everyone else in her peer group seemed to already have it all figured out.

'Ugh, okay, fine. I guess I can talk to you about my crap. But then you will officially become my Amelie surrogate. So no judgement, no scowls and don't give me any advice on how to fix things unless I specifically ask for it.'

Catalina had no idea if this was the right way to go about things, but these were desperate times. She had lost control of basically every aspect of this trip, but at least she could use the opening Theo had provided her with to reclaim some of that control—regardless of whether he knew what he was signing up for.

'I'm here to…find someone,' she said, the words failing her at the very last second.

Theo picked up on the hesitation, his eyebrow

rising in a silent question. Her heart stuttered in her chest when he looked at her like that—or when he looked at her in general, to be honest—and she bit her lip.

Just get it out, she told herself. *You'll feel better with a confidant*. And who knew what could happen from here? Theo had intervened with this creep right now; maybe he could also help her find an acceptable match. It wasn't as if Catalina was looking for her happily-ever-after here. She wouldn't have time for that idea in her life until long after her medical training was done.

What was this woman struggling with? Theo swallowed several barbed responses and fought his inner demons to keep his expression neutral. There was something she was working up to tell him, and even though he couldn't imagine anything to be this nervous about, her hesitation was apparent.

Catalina was here to find someone? A long-lost sibling? A person she'd met while playing an online video game? A missed connection?

The last thought sent a jolt through him, and he pushed it away. It was none of his business who she was here to meet. And he was therefore not entitled to any kind of reaction.

'Okay, this sounds so dumb because I'm twenty-six years old and a whole-ass doctor. Like, I don't even know why I'm telling you this,' Catalina rambled, her nerves obviously getting the better of her.

Theo silenced the part of him that wanted to say something. To assure her she could tell him whatever she wanted and it wouldn't matter. He would still—no. Not a path he could go down, even mentally. His feelings for Catalina—whatever they were—needed to remain unacknowledged, the way they had been over the years of knowing her. So instead he stayed silent, letting her work through whatever mental block she needed to get through.

And if by the end of that she chose to share her thoughts, he would be thrilled. But if she didn't, he needed to be fine with that. Needed to deal with the dread humming at the lower part of his spine.

'When Amelie suggested we do something fun between our internship ending and us choosing our respective fellowship programmes, she came up with the idea of this cruise to force me out of my shell.' She paused, her hand gripping the empty glass in front of her. 'The idea behind it was that since I'll be forced to be on the ship and around people, I might find it easier to…connect with people. It's something I struggled with during med school and also during my internship year. Like, watching *Grey's Anatomy* seriously messed with my head about how much social time junior doctors get.'

'I'm familiar with the workload,' he said, unable to keep the brittleness out of his voice. The stress placed on doctors in training was bad enough. If you combined it with a medical dynasty then it became a time bomb just waiting to explode. Like it had in his life.

'What I'm trying to say here is that, outside of Amelie—and I guess you, to some extent—I didn't hang out with people or get to know anyone or have...*been* with anyone. You know?' She dropped her gaze at the last part, staring at where her fingers connected with the glass as if it was the most interesting thing in here. And, to be fair, it might actually be true, seeing that creep seemed to be the calibre of people coming here.

She hadn't been with... His thoughts ground to a halt, heat blossoming in the pit of his stomach before he could control any of this reaction. Wait, was Catalina really telling him that she'd never been in a relationship? Never been...?

A tendril of awareness—hot and persistent—unfurled in the pit of his stomach, and though he batted it away it remained there, suggesting *something* he had no business entertaining.

'I see.' Theo knew it was the wrong thing to say even as he said it. The sound came out too clinical but somehow also too...curious? A strange divide to straddle, but somehow he had managed it with the efficiency of a contortionist. And here his former girlfriends had all said he wasn't flexible enough. What did they know?

'And this is my chance to catch up. Or at least I thought it was, but you see how that turned out.' Catalina dropped her head, waving in the direction where the guy had run off to.

He still wasn't sure why she was telling him all of this, and a small part of him wished she hadn't. What was he supposed to do with this information? There was nothing *he* could do about it, and yet the thoughts unravelled in his brain as if she'd tugged on a loose strand. Fantasies coalesced in front of him unbidden, and he swallowed several times to get rid of the thickness coating his throat.

'Because of my predicament, I apparently don't even know how to pick them. Like, could I have known Dave was a creep not worthy of even five minutes of conversation?' When she looked back up, Theo had to ball his hand into a fist not to reach out and touch her.

'I promise you he wasn't. Anyone worth your attention doesn't have to beg for it,' he said without thinking, and something in her eyes lit up. The dejection he'd seen there a few moments ago was transforming into a different expression right in front of him.

'Did you know he was a sleaze when you saw us talking?' she asked, eyes wide enough to reflect the strobe lights behind him.

He paused, unsure where this line of questioning was going and whether he really should be the one to follow it to the end. 'I had a pretty good guess,' he admitted.

Her expression turned radiant. Even in the dim light, he could see the energy coming back into her body. Only he couldn't see her like that. It would make staying away from her even harder. Something he'd struggled with during his time in med school until he'd been glad to leave because the constant distraction of Catalina Reyes was finally out of his life. Or at the very least contained to major holidays.

Theo didn't have time for distractions like that, and because he didn't he could not let himself think about how much he might have liked to be distracted. How much fun it might have been. Or if his life might have been different if he'd chosen different priorities.

The cruise was starting to look like a glimpse through a window into a past he had denied himself.

Was that why Amelie had told him to stay away from Catalina?

'How?' Catalina asked, eyes still wide in wonderment.

'How…what?'

'How did you know he was a sleaze?'

Theo blinked several times as his thoughts crashed back into reality. 'What do you mean?'

'Because…look, I think I knew as well. But

I wasn't sure. There was a sinking feeling in my stomach. A sense of impending doom. But I brushed it off because I thought maybe that's my inexperience. What if I'm just uncomfortable with flirting?'

'You're not.' The words were out before he could stop them and as they floated between them, Theo cursed silently. He knew exactly what she was going to ask next, and he had no idea—

'How do you know that?' Yup. There it was.

'Because I've been around you, believe it or not. We might not talk much, but you're far from quiet. You…grab people's attention. And you know how to talk to people. Flirting is just that: talking.' Subtext weighed down his words to the point where anyone else would have called him out on it. But this was Catalina sitting across from him. She'd not once acknowledged what lay beneath the snipes between them, had never even hinted at being interested in more—on the other side of the coin that was their contentious relationship.

Though with what he knew now—and the questions she was asking—he wondered if maybe she genuinely didn't know. That she hadn't picked up what he'd put down all those years ago—not because she hadn't been interested but because… she couldn't tell?

The way she stared at him, mouth as wide as her eyes, it had to be the latter. Which put him in a far more dangerous situation than he'd previously thought. Years ago, he'd believed himself rejected. But what if it wasn't true? Had he mistaken a lack of experience as a hard no? With an ego far bigger than his achievements warranted, Theo had retreated back into the safety of his peer group, where people knew him and appreciated him for who he was—regardless of what he'd *actually* achieved so far.

The way she spoke of their shared past now, he realised Catalina had no idea of his intentions back then. Which, in turn, meant there was a chance.

And Theo couldn't have that. Considering how thoroughly his life was in shambles right now. With his reputation in tatters, any connection to him would only hold her back in her future career. He wouldn't have it on his conscience.

'I do?' Catalina paused, and he wasn't sure if she was speaking to him or to herself. Then he flinched when she clapped her hands, her expression transforming from puzzlement to something steely. Resolved. 'Here's the deal, Theodore. I know how you'll make up for all of this: you'll be my wingman.'

That was not at all what he'd expected to come out of her mouth. It was, in fact, so absurd that he snorted in the most undignified, non-Morgan appropriate fashion. 'Your wingman? You didn't even know the guy was a sleaze. How do you know what a wingman is?' As he asked, he realised the answer and held his hands up. 'My sister, of course.'

'She was supposed to be my wingwoman and land me with someone who can, you know…take care of *it*.'

Another burst of heat rippled through his body, hotter than the previous one, shooting through him and into every extremity. He clenched his jaw to regain control, tamping down on the *thing* inside him that had stirred when he'd first seen her again in the lobby five days ago and which was now projecting ungodly pictures in his mind. Except he didn't see himself in there, but rather the creep—or a loose approximation of him—with Catalina, and the heat turned into something discomfiting. A feeling he couldn't remember ever feeling this intense: jealousy.

What terrible things had he done in a past life that he would be tormented like this? Having Catalina, of all the women on this planet, ask *him* to help her get laid. For the first time. That was knowledge he couldn't un-know now. Nor could he forget how she intended that man to be anyone but him—or how he shouldn't *want* to be him.

It didn't make being around her any easier. Not that he idolised virginity or anything like that. No, simply thinking of her in this way was provoking thoughts he could—*should*—do without.

'I don't think I will.'

In fact, there was no chance in hell Theo was going to do that. He'd already had to employ a breathing technique when he'd seen the guy touch her without her consent. How was he supposed to help her find someone else when he—?

Nope. There was no way he would let himself go there. His silly infatuation—because that was what it was—would stay in the past. Maybe he should help her with her harebrained idea. Just to prove to himself that these lingering thoughts were nothing but a result of their forced proximity. That there was a reason he preferred to stay away from her, and it was because he needed to keep a lid on things.

'You owe me, Theo.' Catalina couldn't hide the wince as she said that, just as he couldn't help the smirk from appearing on his lips.

'How exactly do you figure I owe you?' he asked, now leaning close enough that her scent drifted up his nose. The same hint of lavender he'd caught that first day when he'd stood behind her. A smell he knew was all over the cabin they were supposed to share. The one he hadn't set foot in since showing her the way, because there was no way he could withstand the proximity to Catalina. He would lose his sleep along with what little of his sanity remained.

'Well…it's technically not your fault Amelie fell off a horse and broke her ankle. But, as both an older and a younger sibling, I know there are certain responsibilities that come with being the eldest, and so I'm okay holding you accountable for it.'

Theo couldn't stop the laughter bubbling in his throat. 'You went through an awful lot of mental gymnastics to get to this point.'

Catalina shrugged, but he could see she was trying to fight off a smile. Or maybe he just wanted to see her smile because he enjoyed it too much. Probably a combination of both.

Now was the time to stop the jokes and walk away. They had their fun teasing each other, but avoiding Catalina was still one of his top priorities. Especially since she had a way of eroding his defences—and of late he didn't have very many left. The circumstances of his life had left him scrambling to hold on to *anything*. Who knew what might happen if he let himself slip too far out in these unknown waters?

Not that he *wanted* to. Nope, he definitely didn't.

'Fine, say I agree. What's your plan of attack? What do you need in a wingman?' he asked instead of shutting the entire idea down.

Catalina's lips split into a huge grin that stole all the air from his lungs. 'Yes! I knew I could count on you. There's lots to do. First is, of course, checking out people's vibes. Like, you're already good at observing and judging people. Put that power to good use and weed out anyone I should avoid.' She clapped her hands once, clearly delighted. 'Excellent. Tomorrow night's karaoke at the Sunset Bar. Prime vibe-checking territory. Wear something non-threatening.'

He blinked. 'Non-threatening?'

'You know, less brooding serial killer, more supportive bestie. I can help if you need it.'

Theo scrubbed a hand down his face. What had he just agreed to?

Catalina stood, grabbing her drink and shooting him a look over her shoulder. 'Come on, wingman. Let's go back before the good ones are all taken.'

She didn't wait for him to follow, just strolled off into the blur of lights and music as if she hadn't just handed him a live grenade and walked away smiling.

Theo exhaled slowly and dragged himself to his feet. One night. A bit of recon. He could manage that.

Probably.

Maybe.

God help him.

CHAPTER SIX

Day Eight, at sea

After two successive nights of hunting, Catalina had to admit that her plan to make Theo her wingman in her mission to lose her virginity wasn't working out the way she'd imagined it. In her desperation, and also caught up in the moment of her valiant rescue from sleazy Dave, she hadn't realised the fatal flaw in the plan: Theodore Morgan was far too handsome to be her wingman.

The people in the clubs and bars took one look at him before backing off, not wanting to mess with what they thought was his girlfriend. It didn't help that Theo couldn't get rid of his resting bitch face long enough to talk her up to someone.

So instead of making progress in her virginity-losing quest, she'd mostly hung out with her best friend's brother, talking about the most random things.

Which led her to the second problem in this whole scenario—she was kind of enjoying herself. And by *kind of* Catalina meant she didn't feel as if she was missing out on anything when spending her time with Theo.

Which was bad, right? The innocent crush she'd nursed over the years of knowing him was one thing. Completely harmless by virtue of his being utterly uninterested in her and also because they hung out—what, maybe two hours *a year*? It was easy to forget about this man's magnetism when she rarely saw him.

But now that they were spending more time together—both on and off the clock—things had veered into the uncomfortable range.

'So, no pool for me today?' Sam, the receptionist from her first day, asked, their voice raspy.

'Afraid so, Sam.' Catalina gave them a sympathetic smile. 'You caught a virus from someone. Seems it's going around since you aren't the first here with those symptoms. I'd suggest you lie down for the rest of the day and see how you feel in the morning. Lots of fluids and rest.'

'Why did it have to be on my day off? I—' The rest of their sentence was swallowed by a hacking cough sounding painful enough to make Catalina wince.

She got up from her chair, and Sam followed suit, swaying on their feet as they got off the exam bed. Catalina frowned and stepped closer. 'Will you be okay to get to your cabin?'

Sam gave a slow nod. 'I'll be fine. Thanks, Dr

Reyes.' Catalina opened the door and waved at Sam as they trotted out and down the corridor before disappearing from the clinic.

The sound of coughing hit her before she even stepped out of her office. Catalina frowned, caught off-guard by the muffled chorus echoing from the waiting area. She'd expected maybe one or two more cases before the end of her shift, but as she rounded the corner her jaw dropped.

Every seat in the waiting room was taken. A family of four huddled around a single crossword puzzle, each of them coughing in counterpoint. The two elderly women—chess rivals Catalina had seen battling it out yesterday on the entertainment deck—now sat slumped beside each other with identical boxes of tissues clutched in their laps. Even the normally unflappable bartender from the ship's mid-deck lounge was doubled over, face buried in his hands as if seeing everyone else swaying set him off. Hadn't he been serving her and Theo drinks last night?

She scanned the room, counting. Fifteen. At least half the patients she'd usually see in a day, now assembled all at once and multiplying by the minute. Whatever this respiratory disease was, it spread a lot faster than Catalina liked. Had Theo seen a similar trend? After spending the evening together yesterday, they'd realised this morning they were scheduled together in the clinic as well. Not that they had any time to see each other with the amount of work waiting in the patient room. Also, why would she *want* to see him?

It wasn't as if he could help her pick someone up right now.

No, she wanted to see him because the number of patients still trickling in worried her, and she needed to know if it was appropriate. Theo had worked in one of the largest metropolitan emergency rooms only a few weeks ago. He would know what was going on.

As if her thoughts had summoned him, a door behind her opened and Theo stepped out, along with Dr Chen, heads bowed in discussion. If those two were meeting behind closed doors, there was definitely something wrong.

Catalina stepped forward as soon as she caught Theo's eye, intercepting him before he could disappear back into the staff corridor. Dr Chen had already turned around and vanished behind her office door.

'What's going on?' she asked in a low voice, glancing over her shoulder at the full waiting area. 'I thought this was just a trickle, but it's turning into a flood. This many cases in one day feels… wrong.'

Theo nodded once, his mouth set in a grim line. 'It's a cluster. We've logged twenty-eight symptomatic cases since this morning, and they're all showing the same progression: low-grade fever, dry cough, sore throat, malaise, some with mild dyspnoea. One or two borderline hypoxic, but nothing needing intubation so far.'

Catalina blinked. 'But what *is* it? Influenza?'

'Possibly,' Theo said. 'Could also be adenovirus or parainfluenza, maybe even a seasonal coronavirus strain. We won't know for sure until we get swabs to the mainland. But whatever it is, it's highly contagious. We're looking at a confined-space outbreak—classic cruise ship scenario.'

Her brow furrowed. 'You've seen this before?'

He gave a short nod, rubbing the back of his neck. 'Yeah. We had something almost identical at Morgan Greywater last winter. Two nursing homes got hit at the same time, and we were overflowing within hours. Same presentation, same acceleration. It's the incubation window that screws you—people are contagious *before* they realise they're ill.'

Catalina frowned. 'This is going to be a nightmare.'

He nodded again, glancing over her shoulder towards the waiting room. 'Be extra carcful. Don't take off the mask or those glasses. I can't have you getting sick.'

It was a throwaway line, and Theo couldn't possibly have meant anything by it. Yet her heart still stumbled as the words settled into a squishy place inside her chest. Of course he was worried about her getting sick. She was his colleague in this mess. Plus, he was a doctor and didn't want *anyone* to get sick. This wasn't about her. Except maybe it was, because as it turned out, Theo maybe didn't think she was a piece of gum stuck to his shoe, the way she had always believed. He just had a terminal case of grumpy face.

'W-what are we supposed to do though? Tell them to isolate?' She bit down on her cheek when her hesitation turned into a stutter. Four years of medical school and an additional year as an intern had taught her a lot about being a doctor and how hospitals worked, but this wasn't exactly a regular hospital environment. 'Should we alert the CDC?'

Theo shook his head. 'Dr Chen has already alerted the Maltese health authorities since the ship is registered in Malta. But as the senior medical officer on the ship, she has the authority over how we proceed with this. She's on the phone with the Captain to confirm the plan of action.'

As if his words had summoned her, Dr Chen's office door swung open and she stuck her head out, making eye contact. With a quick wave of her hand, she beckoned them both to enter and when Catalina closed the door behind her, Dr Chen was already sitting back behind her desk.

'Here's what we decided: mild cases will be ordered to self-isolate in their cabin until we reach Dubrovnik tomorrow, at which point we will reevaluate the situation. The Captain decided against turning around and going back to Split port. With how the waiting room is looking right now, I'm expecting more serious cases to come in.' She paused, looking between them. 'I know your shift is supposed to be over soon but, unfortunately, I will require you to stay until the situation is contained. I asked more of the staff to start early as well.'

Next to her, Theo nodded, unsurprised about the decision Dr Chen had made. Was it because he would have made the same decision? Meanwhile, Catalina hadn't even known where to begin triaging, let alone deciding the fate of so many people at the drop of a hat.

'The Captain asked his staff to prepare a room on Deck Four as an overflow in case we need to move critical patients there,' Dr Chen continued when they both stayed quiet.

'Do we have any ICU-grade equipment?' Catalina asked as she played through the scenario in her head. More critical cases would require specialised care—intubation, ventilation, potentially an isolation room.

'We have a few ventilators on board. The crew is currently hauling them out of storage. But it's not—'

'*Help!*' A screech interrupted Dr Chen's words.

Theo was already moving, his long stride swallowing the office in two steps, Catalina tight behind. The waiting room had become a centrifuge of chaos. The bartender, grey-faced, slumped sideways in his chair as his neighbour—a twitchy college kid in a faded Pink Floyd shirt—tried to prop him up while yelling for help.

Theo dropped to his knees beside the bartender, fingers already at the man's wrist. 'Pulse is thready. He's febrile and tachycardic. Catalina—'

'I've got it,' she said, crouching opposite him and pulling on gloves. 'Sir, can you hear me?' She tapped the man's cheek, but he didn't stir. His skin was flushed, sweat clinging to his brow.

'We need to move him.' Theo looked around and spotted a wheelchair. 'Clear the hallway,' he called out, and the crowd shifted without hesitation.

Catalina rolled the chair into place while Theo and the college kid lifted the man in. He slumped to one side, head lolling.

'Hold him steady,' Theo told her, grabbing the handles. 'We'll take him to Exam One. If his breathing worsens, we'll need to start oxygen—maybe prep for escalation.'

Catalina's eyes went wide. 'Do we even have oxygen?' The thought of starting someone on oxygen was so far out from what they'd been told things would be like in the clinic and she couldn't remember whether the orientation day had touched on the subject. Maybe, but she'd been too busy feeling self-conscious about being in the same room as Theo. Great.

'Storage cabinet by the crash trolley,' Theo said

without missing a beat. 'Green cylinder. Regulator should already be attached.'

Right. Catalina spun on her heel and dashed to the cabinet, heart thudding as she yanked the door open. Her fingers hesitated for a split second before closing around the oxygen kit. By the time she turned, Theo had already wheeled the patient into Exam One and lowered the backrest.

'Here.' She passed him the tubing. 'Mask or nasal cannula?'

'Start with a mask. His sats must be dropping fast.'

Catalina connected the tubing, slipped the elastic behind the man's head and adjusted the flow. 'How's he doing?'

'Breathing's shallow, but steady. Chest rising symmetrically, no obvious distress.' Theo placed the pulse oximeter on the man's finger and waited a beat. 'Ninety-one. Not great. Hopefully, it climbs.'

She moved to the IV cart. 'Fluids?'

'Wide open,' he confirmed. 'One litre Ringer's. Let's cool him down too—he's roasting.'

She nodded, grabbing a cool pack from the fridge and wrapping it in a towel before placing it under the man's neck. 'Temp must be sky-high.'

Theo glanced at the thermometer. 'Forty-point-two. Damn. Fever wasn't one of the symptoms I saw on any patient today. You?'

She shook her head while tearing open the

IV kit. 'Nope. Low-grade, maybe, but nothing like this. This could be secondary. Dehydration, maybe?'

'Or an opportunistic infection due to the compromised immune system,' Theo muttered, moving to the cabinet and pulling down a box of antipyretics. 'I'll draw up paracetamol. IV, right?'

'Yeah,' she said, already finding the vein. Her gloved fingers moved steadily now, confidence kicking in. 'Good flashback. Threading.'

Theo turned with the syringe just as she taped the line in place and flushed it. 'Nice stick.'

She smirked. 'Didn't even need a second try. Try not to be too impressed. Us doctors at non-top institutions do just as well.'

'That's not— You think that's how I see you? Like the name of your hospital matters more than how you handle yourself?' Theo let out a laugh and shook his head. Before Catalina could muster a reply, he handed over the paracetamol for her to push through the port. 'Keep an eye on pulse and oxygen. Let's recheck sats, BP and temperature in two minutes.'

As she administered the medication, the heart monitor gave a steady rhythm. No alarms. No panicked spikes.

Catalina exhaled and peeled off her gloves. 'He's stabilising. Colour's better already.'

Theo nodded, eyes still scanning the monitor. 'Breathing's improving too. That oxygen's helping.'

The bartender gave a weak cough and stirred, blinking sluggishly. Theo crouched down beside him, his energy gentle. 'Sir? You're okay. You fainted, but you're stable now.'

The man gave a faint groan in response, eyes fluttering closed again.

Catalina glanced at Theo. 'I guess we'll need to keep a close eye on him?'

'Definitely. I'll radio the crew to see if the room on Deck Four is ready.' He paused, looking at the bartender with a frown. 'Let's keep him in the chair. It's not the most comfortable, but I don't know what the transport situation looks like.'

'Got it. I'll stay and check him over again while we wait for word on what to do next,' she replied with a nod, ignoring the burst of butterflies in her stomach as the adrenaline faded out of her system with the emergency winding down. This persistent feeling should go away, too. Yet it stuck around to annoy her. And made her blurt out the next thing without thinking. 'Look at us. Teamwork.'

She braced herself for his smirk of derision, but when their eyes met, his smile was a lot softer. Or had it always been like that and she hadn't seen it for what it was until now?

His eyes sparkled with amusement. 'Not bad for a girl who forgot where the oxygen was.'

He had not just said that. Catalina huffed out an incredulous laugh and said, 'Not bad for a guy with chronic resting bitch face.'

His smile turned brighter, showing her a flash of the one crooked canine that always caught her attention. 'That's just my neutral.'

'Your neutral scares small children.'

'And yet *you* keep showing up.'

'I don't…' Her voice trailed off when the butterflies in her stomach turned into tiny fireballs, bouncing around her body in an erratic pattern and setting everything they found inside her on fire. Heat prickled at her skin, making it impossible to focus on any single thought she might have. The reply to his words she now couldn't find.

He had noticed her hanging around him despite her own insistence that she shouldn't. But not just that, the implications of his words wormed into her. Had he liked it? Theo certainly hadn't made a concerted effort to avoid her. Except for seemingly finding another place to stay, given he hadn't set foot in their shared cabin after the first day.

A question she still had to ask. Later.

Outside, another cough echoed down the corridor. The next wave was coming, but for a moment they stood in the eye of it—just the two of them, connected by the hum of machines and the steady pulse on the monitor.

Theo hesitated, eyes flicking to her for a beat too long. 'You did well.'

The praise slid under her skin, warm and steady. She shouldn't enjoy his words as much since they didn't mean anything. Who was Theo to her that she would crave his compliment? It was ridiculous how much he fuelled the fire raging within her.

'You're not too bad yourself, Morgan,' she said in an effort to deflect. 'Go radio the team. Patients are piling up, and we need to clear the waiting room.'

Theo gave a quick nod and stepped out, the door swinging shut behind him. Catalina blew out a breath, forcing herself to move. There was no time to stand still and analyse what had just happened. Patients were waiting. Her job wasn't to decode mixed signals—it was to keep people breathing.

Fatigue sat deep in Theo's bones. The only times he'd ever felt anything that was comparable to this level of tiredness had been after long days in the Morgan Greywater boardroom, talking to his parents and the rest of the board about the state of the emergency room. Those were usually followed by nights actually in the ER, making sure his staff members knew he was around. Because he knew what the optics looked like: rich parents appointing their freshly qualified son to a position far beyond his capabilities. He knew the nepotism narrative was impossible to avoid, and he needed to show his mettle to convince the staff he was more than just his family name. Unfortunately for him, that meant stretching himself beyond his means.

With the outbreak of whatever virus had taken hold on the ship, Theo had worked just as hard. But his level of exhaustion was nowhere near similar. Yes, he was tired, but his mind wasn't circling all the problems he hadn't solved or the people he couldn't save.

No, it was quiet in his head as he lay on the lounger on the empty pool deck, staring up at the night sky and scanning the stars as they drifted by.

The pool deck was empty, save for the occasional crew member walking up and down the sides of the ship. Theo had befriended them on his first day here to make sure he could access this part. They had an understanding: the crew would let him spend time alone, and he would be the responsible doctor he claimed to be and not abuse the privilege his crewmates—and new friends—were giving him.

Between these loungers and empty beds in the overflow room next to the clinic, Theo had avoided the shared cabin with Catalina. Though now that the rooms were actually occupied by patients in isolation, he wasn't sure where he would spend his nights.

'You're like weeds, you know that?'

Theo's eyes flew open at the sound of the familiar voice. He hadn't even realised he'd drifted off to sleep. Blinking several times, the blurry figure slowly took on the form of Catalina.

'I'm relentless, even though people try to get rid of me?' he asked, and her chuckle slid down his spine and settled at the base there in a warm buzz.

'Kinda? I more meant I've seen you all day and now that I'm looking for some time alone, there you are.' Catalina hovered over him and even in the dim light of the night sky he could see the exhaustion etched into her features.

They'd worked together until two hours ago, when Dr Chen had finally dismissed them to get some rest. The medical officer's prevailing sentiment was that they had contained most of the virus, but some passengers would be staying in Dubrovnik when they arrived tomorrow, both because they needed the attention only a hospital could give them and to mitigate further risk of spreading.

The crew roster had several built-in redundancies, but even those could run thin if they didn't manage it properly and let some virus eat itself through the ship's population.

'I'm not sure weeds is the right metaphor here. More like a shadow? I follow you wherever you go?' He paused, then sat up enough so there was space at the foot of the lounger for her to sit down. To his surprise, Catalina didn't hesitate before plonking down, her head tipped back in equal, silent wonder at the constellations above them. The hush of the sea and the throb of distant engines were white noise, a perfect buffer against the spooling anxieties neither wanted to examine right now.

She pulled her knees up, arms looped around them. 'Never thought I'd end up pulling an all-nighter as a doctor on a cruise ship,' she said after a minute. 'I mean, I've done night float shifts before, but at least there's a cafeteria and places to hide when you want to scream into the void.'

Theo snorted. 'You could scream now. The only thing that would answer is seagulls.'

She grinned, a slow, tired sunrise of a smile. 'Not my most dramatic breakdown, then.'

Her gaze drifted to him, softer than he'd seen it before, and something in his chest hitched at that. And then it squeezed even tighter when she asked, 'How are you holding up?'

The question caught him off-guard. Not because no one had asked it—Amelie had, countless times, cajoling him to talk instead of turning into an emotional dam—but because he didn't want to lie to Catalina. He realised, in this odd half-life on *The Aurelian*, that he had started to value her opinion more than he wanted to admit. That in a weird turn of fate, he'd found parts of himself he'd thought forever lost, by stepping *away* from his life.

How was it possible when he hadn't even wanted to be here? Something inside him told him the answer lay in the woman sitting next to him. Even with so little contact, Catalina had a way of getting under his skin—flipping some internal switch that left him thinking of nothing but her.

Which was strange, considering the reverse wasn't true for her. She was here actively looking for *someone else*, with his express help. And seemingly unaware of the fact that the thought was killing him inside. Or maybe what was really bothering him was how he was powerless to do anything but help her, now that she was in his orbit.

How he wanted to give her whatever she desired, as long as it wasn't himself.

At least not fully. Small pieces would have to do.

'I'm okay,' he replied, letting the truth settle in between them. That she cared enough to ask meant something. He wasn't sure what, but it was there, a flicker of warmth in a cold place.

'Don't make that face,' Catalina murmured, nudging his knee with her own. 'I can't categorise it, and it freaks me out.'

The air tasted briny, a salty sharpness that was both clean and abrasive, clearing out whatever clouds had settled around him. She looked genuinely concerned, a strange contrast to their default mode of mutual antagonism. He found himself grinning, a small, unguarded twitch that surprised even him.

'I didn't realise I had so many faces,' he said.

'You don't,' she replied, wrapping her arms tighter around her knees. 'Mostly you have "neutral", "I'm judging you" and "Why am I surrounded by idiots?". This one's new.' Her voice softened then, quieter. 'I like it.'

His chest squeezed tight at her words—at how the slight hesitation in them told him all he needed to know about her frame of mind. They'd never sat this close to each other, hadn't ever been this open about, well, anything. It wasn't how their dynamic had worked with Amelie between them acting as a buffer.

Theo had forced himself to keep his feelings hidden beneath an expression of neutrality. Though how Catalina had picked it up had been so much different as he'd learned over the last few days of interacting with her. She'd seen it as disdain.

It couldn't be further from the truth, and that was what made this entire thing so dangerous. He could not let his true feelings out—this was as true now as it always had been and always would be. His sister had been right to warn him away from Catalina.

Yet under the starlight, surrounded by the quiet of the ocean and with the long shift in the clinic wearing down his defences, Theo couldn't muster the usual air of distance. Not when she sat this close, her scent wrapping around him like a soft cocoon. Lulling him into safety.

He leaned in, a thrill running through his body when Catalina didn't flinch.

'I thought the hectic nature of the outbreak would trigger something in me. That it would remind me of how running the ER had ground me down. But it didn't,' he said, the words finding their way out with no resistance. He wanted her to know this, though he couldn't explain why.

Catalina rested her head on top of her folded arms, tilting to the side so their eyes met. 'There was a lot less trauma in that room today. Like, yeah, it was stressful. But I imagine it doesn't compare to the number of high-degree injuries coming into an emergency room like Morgan Greywater. It can't…'

He shook his head as she spoke, her words trailing off before she could finish her sentence. 'It doesn't matter *what* it is. If you feel like you're going to fail, or you're not good enough, that's what gets to you. It's the only thing.'

Catalina stayed quiet for a few seconds before answering him. When it came, her voice was so soft he barely heard it above the lapping of the waves. 'Yeah. I know exactly what you mean.'

Her lips pressed tight, teeth pulling at the inside of her cheek as if she was deciding whether to keep going or shut it all in again. But she kept her eyes on the sky as she went on. 'I used to think that if I was perfect—if I got the grades, did the work, made it into the right schools—my parents would finally notice me. Or at least care about my achievements, you know?' The laugh that followed was brittle. 'Turns out, it didn't matter if I made it to med school or got my name on a plaque. There was always something more impressive my siblings had done. Or some new kid on the way. I couldn't ever be enough.' She shrugged, trying to play it off.

Theo resisted the urge to put his arm around her. Instead, he leaned closer still until their shoulders brushed against each other.

'Going on this cruise and experiencing all these things—it's supposed to be me taking charge of things. Finally living for myself rather than for the expectations of others, you know? Even when it comes to the continuation of my medical training, whenever I look at a path forward, I can't shut up the voice that asks: is this the right way to gain their attention?'

Theo was silent, but it wasn't the uncomfortable hush that sometimes happened when people shared too much. He took a deep breath, exhaling slowly. How had they ended up sharing these things with each other unprompted? 'Sounds like something I need to do as well.'

He wasn't sure how he would even begin to 'live for himself', as she put it. When she'd asked him to help her, something in his chest had stirred. An unease he'd pushed away in denial. If she wanted to meet people it was none of his business. But now that he understood why—understood more of Catalina—the unease came rushing back.

Was that really how she wanted to reclaim her life from whatever ghosts she'd spent chasing all these years? By finding some random guy at a bar? Wouldn't the experience be so much better if he—

The thought was so loud, so intrusive, Theo forgot how to breathe. How could he sit here and continue to support her with her plan when his entire being recoiled from the thought? When in every stray fantasy there was no random guy, but just her with *him*. His mouth exploring her body. His fingers teaching her what pleasure looked like—sounded like.

Dear God, how was he supposed to go through with any of this?

Theo looked at her, the sharp shadow of her profile painted by the distant light of the ship's navigation beacons. She was still, and her expression raw and unguarded in a way he'd never seen before. Maybe she'd never meant to say any of this. Maybe it was the exhaustion, or the hour, or the way the stars went on forever above their heads and nothing felt as heavy as it did during daylight.

But it would be a lie to say he didn't want to be the one to help her rewrite her story. Not as a surrogate or a bystander or a facilitator, but as himself. Theo Morgan, whose entire life had been about denying himself the things he really wanted, because wanting was always dangerous, always selfish, always a threat to the order of things.

He'd spent years telling himself that what he wanted—how he felt about her—didn't matter and would only ever get in the way of the important things in his life. Now, the space between them felt charged as their eyes met, an intense spark jumping between them.

'If anyone would have told me a few weeks ago I'd be sitting with Dr Theodore Morgan on a cruise to stargaze, I don't think I would have believed them,' she said, her voice taking on a quality that sent a trickle of warmth shooting down his spine. She leaned into him now, enough that he could feel her weight against him. So close, he could count her eyelashes, watching their mesmerising dance with each blink.

He huffed a low laugh, wanting to look away but not being able to. If he kept staring at her for much longer, he would forget himself and do something dumb. Act on the attraction that he had felt for her since they'd first met. Because whatever was floating between them now was mutual.

'Yeah, I'm not used to seeing you outside of the rigid programming of our Thanksgiving dinners.'

A smile ghosted across Catalina's lips—soft, a little sideways, part incredulity, part dare. 'We're a lot less horrible with each other than I thought we'd be,' she said. 'Isn't that weird?' The question was half rhetorical; the rest hung between them, open.

'We could fix that,' Theo offered, his voice low. 'We could start bickering again. Re-establish the natural order.'

The silence that followed was long and risky. Theo reached up, brushing a stray curl from the edge of her brow, letting his hand drift just long enough that she could feel the shape of his fingers, the weight of whatever he wasn't saying. It was a deliberate slow-motion act—one that left no room for doubt about intent.

His eyes darted down to Catalina's throat when she swallowed. But she didn't move away from his touch, didn't shift or give him any other indication that he was too close. That he was overstepping. Theo thought he was, knew this wasn't a good idea under these circumstances, or any other. But he couldn't stop himself as his thumb brushed over her cheekbone and a sigh dropped from her lips.

His heart lurched into his throat when she met

his gaze again, eyes ablaze with the same forbidden temptation raising its head in his chest.

'Are you going to kiss me, Theodore, or will you just keep staring at me?'

Something deep in his gut tightened. 'Amelie told me not to.'

She snorted, her nose wrinkled from the effort not to laugh. 'Are you going to listen to her?'

He was both relieved and bereft, because the room for denial had officially closed itself off. Whatever happened next, it was wilful. Chosen. Maybe that was why he hesitated: the old, calcified routine of denying himself in favour of expectations, and the certainty that to want was to set himself up for disaster.

What if he treated his life as suspended here on the ship? Maybe for the duration of his time here, he could be someone else. Try on the skin of a Theo who wasn't so wrapped up in his family's legacy he couldn't escape it. Catalina was looking for someone to give her back control of her life—maybe she could do the same for him?

When he finally leaned forward, it was with a carefulness that was less like hesitation and more reverence for the moment itself. He stopped just shy of her lips.

'You're sure?'

She didn't answer in words. Her hand skimmed the rough line of his jaw, palm cupping the side of his face. There was no tremor—she was as steady as he'd ever seen her.

'Yes,' she said, and that little word made him feel precariously on the edge.

He closed the distance, hesitation burning away in the heat between their mouths. Her lips were soft and tasted like all the fantasies he'd quietly indulged in the time he'd known her. Her body angled towards him on nothing but instinct, pressing into him with a needy, tentative certainty.

He felt himself smiling against her mouth, all the tension of the day evaporating as she kissed him back, equal parts desperate and giddy. The electric charge between them broke as their bodies met, following the rhythm of their bodies. Time seemed to slow when they touched, and the more of *her* Theo got to feel under his hands, the more intoxicated he became.

Theo threaded his hands through her hair, a zing of electricity shooting through him when her low moan reached his ears. Catalina clawed at him, fingers finding purchase in his shirt, and as she pushed towards him, he lay down, pulling her with him until he was flat on the lounger with her straddling him.

The weight and motion of her hips sent a searing jolt from his chest straight to his groin, and for a suspended second Theo was no longer the master of anything—not his body, not his brain, not the wild animal thrum of desire that made his world tilt. He could feel her through the thin summery fabric of her skirt, and all at once his self-control, the one thing he'd always believed in, snapped like a brittle leash, and the friction made him dizzy.

His hands found their way to her hips, relishing the feel of her bare skin against his fingertips when he found the exposed strip of flesh where her shirt was riding up. Was this really about to happen? For years, Theo had imagined what it would be like—fantasising about his complete surrender to this woman who he could never have.

His want had never been an active thing or something he pursued in his life, but rather a slow boil, constantly there in the back of his mind, and he'd lived with the idea that it was all he would ever get. Their lives had diverged before they had even met, and with his future entirely wrapped up in the world his parents had created for him, he knew he couldn't have her. Someone as ambitious as Catalina would have choked in his world.

Only this world wasn't his any more. So maybe he could have her, even if it was just for the duration of this cruise.

The thoughts dispersed when Catalina let out another throaty moan, her hips jerking against him and building the hardness there. The pressure was so unexpected—*delicious*—his head lolled back, making impact with the cheap plastic of the lounger.

Her thighs tensing on either side of his body sent another ripple of pleasure through him, and he surged up, wanting to drag her back onto his mouth and continue down the inevitable path they'd chosen. Only Catalina's eyes were no longer hooded with desire but wide enough for the starlight to bounce off them in a sparkle. Her body was no longer pliant under his touch but rigid.

'Cat…are you…?' He let the words hang in the air because he didn't know how to complete the sentence. His heart, still racing from their kiss, took on a completely different beat, one reflecting the mounting panic he could see in her eyes.

Catalina scrambled off him as if she'd been burned, knees wobbling slightly as she stepped back. Her hands flew to her hair, pushing it back from her face in quick, agitated motions.

Theo sat up, heart still hammering, the sudden chill of her absence making every inch of his body feel exposed.

'Cat?' he said quietly, careful not to spook her further. 'Hey. It's okay.'

She shook her head fast and jerky, as if she was trying to shake something loose. 'I… I shouldn't have—this was a bad idea.' Her voice cracked around the words, the earlier warmth and teasing entirely gone. In its place was a brittleness that made something cold bloom in his chest.

She pressed her palm to her lips, as if to keep anything else from escaping. 'We shouldn't,' she said, voice thin. 'I don't know what I'm doing, I don't—' She cut off, brows knitting as she stared at the deck between her feet. 'Everything is so… We're both… This isn't smart.' She let out a shaky exhale caught between a laugh and a sob.

Theo nodded before she could finish, already feeling the undertow of regret. 'Okay,' he said, giving her the route out. 'You're right.' He forced a steadiness into his voice, the same tone he'd used to call time of death or break bad news to a patient's family. Clinical, because that was how their relationship should be. 'We don't have to—none of this has to mean anything. Just something that happened after a day of high stress, which messed with our judgement.'

Catalina remained quiet, teeth biting into her bottom lip so hard he was sure she'd leave a mark. Then, without another word, she turned and fled across the deck, the sound of her sandals slapping solitary against the composite planks.

Theo couldn't move, too thrown by the events leading up to all of this. He waited until he'd lost track of time. The sea wind picked up as the hour deepened, bringing with it a chill that cut through the humidity. When he finally let himself collapse back onto the lounger, arms splayed and chest rising and falling in uneven increments, the world felt hollowed out.

CHAPTER SEVEN

Day Nine, Dubrovnik

'I MADE OUT with your brother.' The words were both a whisper and a scream, the syllables all fusing together until her sentence became a garbled mess of words.

Amelie peered up at her from Catalina's phone screen, eyes wide as saucers. Her lips parted, then moved wordlessly. Catalina's insides wound tighter with every second of silence ticking by, and she forced herself not to fidget in her chair.

Amelie's entire face lit up in real time. The shriek that followed was so loud Catalina had to jerk one earbud out or risk permanent cochlear damage. She recovered just in time to see Amelie's excitement collapse into a fit of delighted giggles as she pounded a triumphant fist into her mountain of pillows.

'You did *what*?' Amelie's voice rose an octave, and the joy was so unfiltered, so completely uncontained, Catalina didn't know how to process it. Amelie was happy about it? Of all the reactions she had mentally prepared herself for, this one hadn't even occurred to her.

'But you said...' Her voice trailed off as she thought back to several conversations she'd had with her best friend leading up to the cruise, and none of them had involved Theo. Other than the conversation they'd had about Amelie's poorly timed horse-riding debut, all the advice her best friend had given her before her voyage had very much centred around Catalina's need to break out of her own lane and try something new.

Theo hadn't been more than a footnote to that. But then why—?

'You didn't tell me to stay away from him,' she said, levelling an accusing glare at Amelie. Her best friend tilted her head to the side, giving an excellent impression of an owl as she blinked her big eyes.

'No, why would I do that?' she asked, the picture of innocence.

'But you told *him* to stay away from me.' It was what he'd said last night. In the moment, Catalina hadn't even questioned it. Having several siblings, she was more than aware of the dynamics and the specific rules she had to obey as a sister. Even though her relationship with her siblings was more akin to that between rivals, she knew some things were taboo even with the Reyes clan.

Only she would have expected to receive the

same warning, given Amelie knew everything about their proximity and how much time they'd be forced to spend together—more willingly as the cruise went on.

Amelie looked somewhere off to the side, a sly smile accompanying the rosy blush crawling up her cheeks. 'Okay, listen…'

'Why did you tell him to stay away from me?'

'Because…' Amelie let out a sigh. 'I know my brother, and after everything that's happened to him, he needs to let loose a little. A part of me actually believes that breaking my ankle is some divine intervention on my brother's behalf. So he would be forced to leave his house, go on a cruise and actually be around some people. Work a job that is *not* destroying him.'

Catalina frowned. 'Okay, but then why tell him to stay away from me? I could have helped him "let loose", as you put it.' In fact, she was. But now she was wondering how Amelie's command to stay clear of her played into it.

'It's hard to explain. I just know my brother. If I hadn't told him something like that, it wouldn't have even occurred to him he *could* hang out with you. He would have just done his shifts, returned to his bed, rinse and repeat. Even just mentioning you put a dent in that plan.' Amelie shrugged. 'And I was right, wasn't I? Though I thought maybe you'd take him sightseeing, not suck face.'

Amelie burst out laughing when Catalina made

a face at her words, and the sound was so infectious she joined in despite herself.

'So what I'm hearing is you basically pimped me out to your brother to get him out of his funk. Are you also planning on letting him take care of my little problem?'

Her best friend screwed her eyes shut. 'Ew, no. Or like, if you really need to, fine. But then we just found the first thing you and I can't talk about openly, because there is no way I will survive hearing about you and my brother doing it.'

Heat burst alive inside Catalina when her thoughts wandered down the path Amelie didn't want to discuss. Last night had not gone the way she'd expected. When she'd headed up to the pool deck, she had been looking for fresh air and a moment alone with her thoughts that wasn't inside her dim cabin.

But seeing Theo under the starlight, alone and so obviously untethered, she'd ended up sitting beside him. And then—God, she'd lost herself in the hush and the heat and the undeniable pull between them. It had been perfect. And then, less than a second after it started to feel real, she'd vaporised the moment. Sunk deep into her own panic and bolted.

She could still feel the press of his hands on her hips, the rough drag of his beard along the corner of her jaw, the way he'd asked if she was sure. It was only after she'd fled—like a cartoon character leaving a dust cloud and debris in her wake—that the shame had set in. She had chickened out, and not for the first time during this trip. Theo had been right there, his desire for her undeniable, and something within her had balked at it.

The confirmation of the knowledge that her one-sided crush hadn't been, well, one-sided had thrown her for a loop. When had that happened? She thought back to the moments they'd shared throughout the years, none of them standing out to her. He'd always been this brooding, unapproachable presence to her.

This development had to be more recent, right? Maybe as recent as the cruise. With what had happened to him back in the States, that would explain it. Weren't people more prone to rash decisions after a major life event?

This could be an opportunity she hadn't even realised she'd been waiting for.

Amelie's shocked gasp sounded metallic through the phone's speakers. 'Oh my God, you *like* him. I don't know if I should say *aw* or *ew*.'

Catalina bristled, her defences kicking in without her input. 'Girl, you've always known I had a crush on him.'

'Yeah, but I thought it was like my crush on Adam Sandler. Not like a *real* thing. How can you like Theo? He's literally the worst.'

Catalina rolled her eyes, but her pulse thudded in her neck. 'He's not always the worst,' she muttered, and instantly regretted how plaintive it sounded.

‘Gag. That’s even worse! Now you see him doing, like, normal human things and you’re in love?’ Amelie clapped a pillow to her face, but not before Catalina caught the smile crimping at the corners of her mouth.

‘That’s…not… I mean—’ She fumbled, mortified by the flash of heat rising through her cheeks. ‘We didn’t actually do anything, okay?’

‘But you wanted to.’ It wasn’t a question.

Catalina closed her eyes, letting her breath escape in a hiss. ‘No! *Maybe*. I panicked, and now I don’t know how to be around him.’

Now, to be fair, she hadn’t exactly been confronted with him today. Come to think of it, she *still* didn’t know where he had been spending his nights. She’d meant to ask him on the pool deck last night but they had got…distracted. He’d said things she couldn’t stop thinking about. Had opened up about what the pressure of his family name had done to him. And she’d shared things with him only Amelie knew. The closeness had wrapped around her like a fog, making her forget who was actually sitting in front of her—and how far-fetched the thought of them together really was.

Above her, the ship’s PA system whirred to life, announcing their imminent arrival in Dubrovnik. With a sigh, Catalina sat up. ‘Listen, I know you had fun with this. But it was a mistake. A moment of weakness after a long shift that had left both of us feeling vulnerable. Nothing serious has or will happen between me and your brother.'

Going by Amelie's unimpressed expression, she didn't believe a word she'd said. 'Right.'

'And to prove it to you, I will go to Dubrovnik today and mingle—for real, this time. No Theo to ruin me for potential single men with his brooding presence.'

'Now that's the spirit.' Amelie perched higher on her pillow tower, tucking a leg beneath her as if settling in to a grand saga. 'Go forth and sow your wild oats, Cat. I want a ten-photo minimum. Extra points if you get at least one hot local to buy you a drink.'

Catalina snorted, waved goodbye and then ended the call.

By the time she made it off the gangway and onto Croatian soil, the sun was already bruising the sky over Dubrovnik's terracotta rooftops. Catalina stood at the edge of the old port and tried to summon an emotion other than exhaustion or a vague sense of cosmic embarrassment. The city shimmered, beautiful in a way that felt almost staged—white limestone walls, bougainvillea, alleys paved with centuries of intent. She wanted to feel something: thrill, wanderlust, even loneliness would do. Instead, all she could feel was the imprint of Theo's hands on her hips, the press of his mouth, the impossible ease of their conversation as they'd stargazed on the pool deck.

She'd spent all morning bracing herself for a run-in. Maybe he'd be on the shuttle bus into the city, or at the breakfast buffet, or in the queue for Customs. But he'd vanished. She'd spent the entire ride craning her neck to spot him, convinced that at any moment he'd materialise, looming and silent. Instead, she'd ended up sandwiched between a bachelorette party from Leeds and a pair of elderly German tourists who'd spent the entire trip arguing over which *Game of Thrones* episodes had been filmed on location.

Catalina tried to enjoy the city despite herself. She wound her way through the old town, checking off the list she'd put together to distract herself—*Walk the walls. Find a dragon egg. Buy a fridge magnet*—and even managed to grab a coffee at a tiny bar tucked into an alley, where the server spoke five languages and insisted she try the local fig liqueur 'for luck'.

She was at Pile Gate, eyes closed and letting the late-afternoon sun coat her skin, when a voice behind her said, 'Melanin is not a force field, you know? You have to wear SP. I can see you're beginning to burn.'

It was so perfectly him that Catalina's heart skipped hard enough to leave her dizzy. She turned, and there he was: Theo in simple jeans and a navy shirt, the sleeves rolled up to show the muscles in his forearms, his hair messily windswept and his face clean-shaven for the first time since they'd boarded.

'You shaved.' She blurted the words out, the vision such a stark contrast from last night. The rough hair had abraded her skin, mixing pleasure with pain as they'd deepened the kiss. The memory was enough to summon the unwanted desire she'd been fighting all day—and all night before that.

His hand came up to his face, rubbing his cheeks. The corner of his mouth kicked up in a boyish smile. 'It was time for the beard to go.'

'How come?' She missed it. That was weird, right? She'd yelled at him about how hideous it was, yet eight days had somehow been enough to change her picture of him. Or maybe it had more to do with the fact that she now knew what it felt like against her skin.

Theo dropped his gaze down to his shoes, nudging a tiny rock before looking back up. When he did, a slice of vulnerability flashed in his eyes—the same thing she'd seen last night. It lasted no more than a second before it disappeared, leaving the usual mask of indifference in place.

'It was time to let go.'

'Oh...'

Her throat squeezed at the admission, and for a heartbeat she thought he might actually say more.

That he'd lay it all bare, the thing that had been simmering just beneath the surface since…since always? Maybe she should say something? Tell him that last night had been a mistake. Fun up until the point where she'd bolted, but still a mistake.

'How are you enjoying Dubrovnik?' she asked instead, feeling like a right chicken as they fell into a slow walk.

'Not bad,' he said, and the words drifted lazily between them. 'I didn't expect much, but the city's beautiful. Even the air smells different here.' He seemed distracted, or maybe just uncertain—his hands kept finding and leaving his pockets.

Catalina tried to orient herself, to find the familiar tension, the old comfort of their mutual antagonism. It stubbornly refused to surface.

'What does it smell like?' she asked.

Theo considered the question, then shrugged, glancing over at her. 'Stone. Sea. And a little like burnt sugar. I passed at least three gelato places.'

'Don't tempt me,' she muttered, then caught herself. 'I'm trying to pace myself after the local speciality coffee that was more sugar than coffee. And a fig liqueur the bartender swore would change my life.'

'Did it?'

Catalina shrugged, trying her best to ignore the tension following their words. They had to address it, right? That was the reason her stomach wound itself into a tight knot with every step they took, immune to the Croatian beauty surrounding them?

'Jury's still out. It spiked my blood sugar and it's giving me some cravings. Not the worst problem to have in Dubrovnik.'

'Did you eat already?' He didn't look at her as he spoke, walking forward with the confidence of someone who knew where they were going. Catalina, meanwhile, was so frazzled by his appearance, she wasn't able to do more than follow—not even contemplating where he might lead her.

'Just some snacks here and there. I didn't feel like sitting down and having a whole meal. Too…' Her voice trailed off when she realised what she'd been about to say.

Was there a chance Theo would let her get away with this? Her stomach did another loop when his head tipped to give her a sidelong glance. 'Too what?'

I'm too freaked out about us making out, and if I stop for even one second, that's all I can think about. The words were right there in her amygdala, along with all the other stuff Theo brought forth in her. But she wouldn't say them. No, that would be weird.

So yeah, she might have figured out that her crush was a bit more reciprocated than she'd thought it would be. Not a big deal. Except in all those years, Catalina hadn't even once entertained the idea of acting on said crush. A part of her was busy convincing herself the reason for it was because Theo was her best friend's brother. Forbidden fruit.

But now that they had stepped over the line she'd never thought they'd cross, she had to admit her reluctance had come from a different place: his obvious dislike of her.

Only that idea lay in tatters at her feet, his desire for her so clear it had freaked her out and beaten her into a retreat that was still causing her no small amount of embarrassment.

'I feel a bit…frazzled,' she ended up saying, lacking the proper vocabulary to say—or rather *avoid* saying—what she really wanted to say.

Theo, of course, didn't let the matter drop. 'Frazzled?' he repeated, head tilting to the side in such a familiar way she now couldn't see the gesture without seeing him, too.

'That's the most accurate word I can come up with, Theo. Take it or leave it.'

They continued to walk in silence, the low mumbling of the surrounding people wrapping around them. Her steps were aimless, her brain wiped clean of her intended itinerary and simply following the street one step at a time. Or maybe she was following Theo, even though she had no idea why. They'd said what they were willing to say—which evidently wasn't a lot—so they should go their own ways again. Slip back into what their relationship used to be before the kiss. Before this entire cruise.

'Are you okay?' They'd reached a quiet viewing platform overlooking the port, and they stood there, watching throngs of people boarding the ship again.

Theo's words took a few seconds to register as Catalina disentangled herself from her thoughts. She blinked a couple of times and then looked up at him. Nope. That was a mistake. With the beard gone, his handsomeness had evolved to a new level. Not that she didn't like the beard. The feel of it still lingered on her skin, invading her thoughts whenever she let them drift too far from the safe zone.

'Yeah, I am…' Catalina gave the words a moment to sink in and become the truth through sheer willpower. They did not. Before Theo could say anything else, she hung her head and let out a deep sigh. 'No, I'm not. I'm not—'

Catalina's whole body tensed so hard she could feel the muscles twitch in her legs. She hugged her arms to her ribcage and blurted, 'I'm sorry about last night.'

Theo's lips parted; she watched the words hit him, watched his eyes flicker with too many emotions to interpret. She pushed on before he could respond. 'I know I was telling you all these things about what I'm hoping to get out of this cruise and how you should help me. But I didn't mean… I wasn't talking about *you* doing all of…ugh.'

Theo stilled beside her, his focus so sharp she felt its pressure on her skin. She expected a quip, a smug arch of brow, proof he'd won some private game she'd never agreed to play. Instead, when he spoke, his voice had a distant quality to it.

'Don't apologise. This is on me. I promised to be your wingman and I should have stuck to that. I shouldn't have let myself get carried away. It was a long day, and I shouldn't have put all of my problems on you. Or kissed you.'

Yes, of course. That made sense. Catalina had struggled with the same thoughts of vulnerability all day, leading her around the city without actually taking it in. His words should be the relief she'd been chasing. The confirmation that even though something had happened, it wasn't a big deal. Nothing had been broken between them, and they could go back to their normal ways where they repelled each other like oil and water. Where the most he had to tell her was a snide comment here and there. Where she didn't have to contemplate if he maybe liked her too.

So why did his words press down on her, making it harder to breathe? What was that sludge-like substance her blood had turned into? Catalina knew what it couldn't be: regret.

'Okay, cool…yeah. Sounds like we are on the same page.' She struggled through those words, finding them somewhere in the back of her brain, and because of that they didn't sound sincere or even real.

Theo picked up on it, too. A line appeared between his brows, and when his gaze swept up and down her entire form, a shiver crawled down her spine. The concern in his eyes was clear, but it came with a flavour of something else that contradicted what he'd just said. A hunger that had been clawing at her for longer than she was willing to admit.

'Where are you sleeping?' Catalina blurted the words out, the question the first thing that came into her head as she looked for a distraction from the searing heat his eyes raised in her.

Something inside her squirmed when she saw the surprise ripple over his expression. Not often could she surprise him, but the question kept nagging at her whenever she settled down in the cabin, waiting for the door to open. All the nights leading up to yesterday, the thought had filled her with quiet unease. Last night, however…

Theo looked down at his shoes again, a gesture more familiar by the day. She'd always thought of him as stalwart—unshakable. But even without knowing what she knew from Amelie, she could see beyond the abrasive façade now. See the man behind the figure he'd created to keep himself safe. Sane.

'You noticed my absence?' he asked, and was

there a flirty tone to his voice, or was Catalina's desperate brain conjuring things? Hadn't they just agreed that the kiss—and any potential additions—had been a mistake?

'Given you are quite…um, noticeable…yes. I did *notice* that a seven-foot tall man did not show up in my cabin every night.'

A thrill went through her as he looked back up and the corner of his mouth kicked up in a half-smile. 'I'm six foot five.'

She pursed her lips. 'I rounded up.'

'I hope you don't round this liberally with your prescriptions.' Now his lips split in a smirk, sending her heart rushing through her body.

'I—well, of course not. I'm a fully qualified doctor even if I haven't decided on a specialty yet.' Catalina's voice came out more breathless than sharp, betraying her lack of composure. This was the other thorn in her side—her complete lack of motivation to find a residency and continue her training.

Which was so unlike her, who had competed for first place in everything she'd done all her life. Where was that competitive spirit when it came to her career now?

'Good. Just checking.' He shifted his weight, shoulders relaxing, and somehow the tension that had bound them for the last several minutes just… disappeared. She saw it in the way his mouth softened, in the way he tucked his hands into his pockets and angled his body towards hers, not away.

They stood that way for a long moment, neither of them willing to break the fragile truce, until finally Theo said, 'So are we good?'

Catalina took a breath, then another, and found that the answer was yes—even if she still didn't fully understand what 'good' meant for them. 'We're good.' She even managed a small smile and hoped it was convincing. 'If you tell me where you've been staying. Your refusal to answer the question is concerning.'

Theo sighed and shook his head. 'You're really going to drag it out of me, aren't you?' His words carried an undertone of admonishment, but then he continued, 'I'm not avoiding the question for any nefarious reasons. I just… Amelie clearly didn't think this swap through in its entirety, and I didn't want to be a presence in your personal space when I know you don't want me there.'

Catalina's first instinct was to insist that she didn't mind having him in her space. That he'd been wrong to assume she wanted him as far away as possible from her. But she couldn't say it because it would put her across the boundary they'd just re-established. The more distance there was between them, the better.

'I appreciate it,' she said instead, giving him a small smile. 'But this still doesn't answer my question. Like, have you been sleeping on the loungers on the pool deck all this time?'

Catalina laughed as she said it, going for the most absurd scenario she could come up with. Sure, he'd wanted to make her feel safe, but even Theo wouldn't go to such lengths.

He didn't laugh. Didn't say anything, either. His mouth twitched as if caught between a smile and a frown, and as the silence stretched between them, Catalina gasped. 'You did not!'

'Not that often on the pool deck,' Theo said, raising his hands in defence.

'Oh, but in other parts of the ship? Have you been sneaking into the cinema at night, living there like a stowaway?' There was no way Theo had done that, right? He would have arranged his own cabin.

'No, not the cinema. I don't think that would have been particularly comfortable.' He gave another shake of his head, and she could see the different thoughts rippling over his face. Theo was debating whether he should tell her. But why would he…?

'Until yesterday, I was mainly staying in the little hospital-like room we're now using to isolate worse cases of the virus,' he said, voice low as if he had to force himself to speak.

'Theodore!'

'It's *fine*. They didn't have any empty cabins, so I made do with it. I didn't tell you because you don't need to worry about it. Okay? I got it covered.'

Her brain short-circuited, skipping every reasonable follow-up and landing on the most indelicate one. 'Wait—how have you been showering?' The words came out before she'd realised she was thinking them, and the flush of embarrassment hit her half a second too late to reconsider her words.

A slow smile crept across his mouth. 'The gym's open twenty-four hours. I use the crew showers there.' He shrugged, as if the image of Theo, alone at three a.m. towelling off under the fluorescent lights, was entirely mundane.

It was not. It was really, really not.

'Oh my God. You really are a stowaway,' Catalina said, but it came out more fond than frustrated. 'You can't keep living like that for almost two more weeks, Theo. You're coming back to the cabin.'

The invitation came out with far less resistance than she'd expected. Because at the very front of her mind she knew with absolute certainty she couldn't have Theo Morgan next to her in bed. The split second she took right now to consider her proposal was enough to fill her head with all sorts of ideas and pictures she knew she needed to stay away from.

Yet she didn't take the offer back. Everything about Theo might spell danger to her, but she couldn't leave him to sleep on a lounger on the pool deck all night. Or worse, have him sneak into the quarantine ward and risk getting sick himself.

'Cat—'

She knew that stern expression far too well and shook her head.

'Nope. Don't argue with me, Theo. I know you are trying to be considerate, and I appreciate it. But this is not an adult solution. We can *share* a room without issues. Right?'

He hesitated. She could see the calculation of reluctance on his face before the words arrived. 'If you're sure.'

'I'm sure,' she said, more firmly than she felt. 'No drama, no tension. We're both adults. And besides, Amelie would murder me if she knew I'd let you sleep in the quarantine room instead of a real bed.'

Catalina owed him this measure of consideration even if it made her squirm. He had dutifully gone out with her a couple of times and played her wingman, even if he'd done a poor job of it. Catalina might be hyper-competitive and always looking for the challenge in anything she did, but that didn't mean she wouldn't look out for others. Maybe it was her ultimate flaw, having always put herself second whenever her siblings had needed something. She had somehow set the precedent of being a third parent to both her older and younger siblings, taking care of all the things they needed.

Never being asked what she needed. To the

point where she now didn't know how to continue her life when it was time to put her needs first.

Or maybe the challenge here would be how to resist Theo while still chasing the fun she'd come here for. Ugh, when had this become so complicated?

'But no shenanigans,' she said, glaring at him even though the words were meant for herself.

Theo's mouth quirked. 'No shenanigans,' he agreed solemnly, as if swearing the Hippocratic Oath again.

'Great. Settled.' Catalina exhaled all the pent-up nerves like a diver coming up for air. 'Now that you're officially not homeless, let's get moving. Ship's leaving in, what, two hours?' She checked her phone and did a double-take. 'Forty-five minutes. Crap.'

They both glanced at the port, then at the warren of alleys winding down towards the water, and realised they had quite a way to go to reach the ship. With no further ceremony, Catalina whirled around and strode towards where Theo stood, when her foot caught on an uneven cobblestone.

The world tilted beneath her as she lost her balance, falling face first towards the ground.

She didn't have time to brace or even panic. Two strong hands closed around her waist, righting her with a jolt that slammed her back against the wall of Theo's chest. For a breathless second she felt his pulse thundering against her spine, the heat of him steadying her as if they were the only two people in the city. His arms didn't let go immediately; instead, one palm hovered at her ribs, the other settling just above her hip, anchoring her with a gentleness she'd only recently learned was so *him*.

'You okay?' His voice was low, soothing her panic even as embarrassment spiked through her.

'Yeah, I just—' She tried to laugh off the humiliation, but it came out shaky. 'I guess I got too excited about going back to our shoebox cabin.'

Theo's hand lingered. If she'd wanted to escape, she could have. Instead, she stood there, half-turned in his arms, her own hands braced on the flat planes of his chest. So close, their breaths mingled. She'd never realised how much softer his mouth looked without the beard, or how the new smoothness sharpened the lines of his jaw, made all that intensity feel exposed and dangerous.

His eyes flickered down to her lips, then up again, searching for permission.

Catalina should not give it. They'd just agreed to no shenanigans, and standing this close to him had to fall in that category, right? Plausible deniability had stopped the moment neither of them hadn't immediately moved away after righting her.

But instead of doing that, she pushed her chin out, enough to close the distance between their mouths and give Theo the consent he'd been asking for.

Her eyes fluttered closed when his warm breath grazed her cheeks, and her heart lurched, bracing for his touch with a giddiness inappropriate for what they were about to do.

Except this time, Theo didn't close the distance. The expectation built, balancing on a knife edge, and then—he ducked his head, brushing his lips against her forehead instead. It was brief, featherlight, barely contact at all. When he drew back, his hands fell away, a careful step creating enough space that the cold air rushed in between their bodies.

'We should go,' he said softly, voice so low she almost didn't catch it. There wasn't a trace of mockery or indifference, just a complicated knot of longing and regret, the kind of gravity that threatened to pull her straight under if she let herself look too hard.

She wanted to say something—anything—that would make sense of the whiplash between her pulse and what he'd just done. Catalina couldn't decide if she was relieved or devastated.

But she just nodded, following a step behind Theo as they walked the winding alleys of Dubrovnik back to the shuttle that would get them to port.

CHAPTER EIGHT

Day Ten, at sea

THE DRONING OF the bass was particularly obnoxious tonight. Or maybe it was Theo's mood. Or perhaps his general dislike of literally everything might have to do with Catalina standing at the bar and talking to some guy who clearly saw her more as an object than a person.

Not that it was any of his business. Theo was supposed to be her wingman. Talk her up to potential matches and then make himself scarce. Right now, the scarce bit was the only one he was following. In fact, he wasn't entirely sure if Catalina even knew he was here—watching like some kind of love-sick creep. How could he even tell her who would be a good match if he himself was resorting to such behaviour?

Hanging his head, he looked down at the half-empty beer bottle. His finger rubbed along the label until a corner of it peeled off, leaving a sticky residue behind.

He needed to get a grip on himself. After Dubrovnik, they'd come to a tentative truce and the agreement not to let any of their hormone-driven feelings get ahead of them. Unlike strangers on a cruise, they would still be in each other's life in some capacity. Though after what had happened at Morgan Greywater, he didn't know what that would look like. Would he ever again be welcome at his parents' home? Amelie had been able to form a relationship with them despite her refusal to have anything to do with the family legacy. But she'd made that choice early on, rejecting the name and all it entailed to pursue her own happiness.

His parents had been sceptical back then, but had quickly shifted their attention back to their son. His failure to live up to expectations wouldn't go down as easily. They hadn't even reached out to him since he'd walked out of his office, never to return.

'This is what you do for fun? Brooding?' Theo looked up as Dr Chen slid into the chair opposite his, holding her own drink in her hand.

'Dr Chen, good to see you,' he said, but the woman shook her head.

'Please call me Sarah. I'm all for reporting structure, but neither of us is working right now,' she said with a smile infectious enough that Theo felt his own lips twitch.

'Very well, Sarah. How are things?' He gave

her a cursory glance, surprised by how different she looked outside the clinic. They hadn't ever interacted when it wasn't about work, and he hadn't even considered socialising with her until the moment she'd sat down. Truth be told, he still wasn't in the mood to talk to anyone as his eyes kept flitting back to where Catalina stood, leaning against the bar, talking to…whoever that was.

'Good. Enjoying some time off for once. The situation with the virus is somewhat contained now, thank God. We had to disembark so many people and transfer them to the hospitals in Dubrovnik to reduce the risk for the passengers but, as you can see, things have been much calmer today,' she said, settling back in the chair and letting out a sigh. 'I thought it was about high time I came out for a bit, and imagine my surprise when I found you brooding here.'

Theo bristled at her words, though he wasn't sure why. Objectively speaking, he *was* brooding. Even he could acknowledge his mood. He just wasn't keen on talking about the why of it, and he got the feeling that was what Sarah was here to do.

She surprised him again when she said, 'So, Morgan Greywater? Not often we get such a big name to join us on a cruise.'

His stomach flipped over, muscles tensing at the mention of the hospital that had cost him so much.

'Not what I was planning on doing after leaving my position. You know my sister was supposed to be here.'

Sarah chuckled. 'Yes, and the only reason I even agreed to such a controversial swap was because of the guarantee your name carries. It doesn't mean much to the cruise as a whole, but I've read the articles you've published.' She paused, giving him a well-meaning smile. 'Doctors usually don't get to send someone else just because they can't make it.'

Of course, his being here was somehow another twist of the privilege his name brought. It was the thing people saw when they learned his last name—the fame and the doors it might open. No one took even a moment to look beyond and acknowledge the pressure that came with it. How much the name *Morgan* demanded on a personal level.

All the smoke and mirrors had ultimately led to his cracking.

'I appreciate your flexibility,' Theo replied, voice clipped despite himself.

Sarah tilted her head, studying him. 'May I ask you a personal question?'

He furrowed his brow, but gave a nod for her to continue.

'Why did you accept the swap? I understand helping your sister, but it's not like your family couldn't afford the contract penalty associated with a last-minute cancellation. Don't get me wrong; your work is excellent. I just don't get the feeling you want to be here.'

He let out a soft breath, gaze slipping past her to the dance floor, where Catalina's laugh rang out above the club noise. 'I didn't come here to enjoy myself, no.'

'So why come at all?'

Her direct question drew his gaze back to her, his mind stalling when he couldn't come up with an immediate answer. It should be clear to anyone *why* he'd come—including himself.

'My sister needed my help.'

His mouth snapped shut when Sarah shook her head.

'No, we've been over this. With who you two are, no one *needed* anything. So, try again. Why did you even bother to come here?'

Theo bristled, his pride making him want to push against Sarah and turn the question around on her. Who was she to him to even ask these questions? They weren't friends just because they worked together—and even that was a stretch. Most of the time Theo spent on his own in one of the exam rooms.

His jaw muscles tensed, molars grinding against each other as he shut those thoughts down one by one. Why was he reacting like this to what was only an innocent question? Sure, one that was designed to uncover more of him, but he reminded himself that colleagues *liked* to get to know each other better. Just because he'd been raised from early on to see everyone as competition didn't mean others functioned the same way.

Hadn't he spent the time after quitting trying to de-program himself from all those things his parents had forced on him?

'This offer arrived when I was craving a change. It seemed wrong to refuse just because cruise ships aren't all that appealing to me when I didn't specify *what* change I wanted to see.' The words got as close to the truth as he felt comfortable with.

Catalina's laugh reached his ears again, the sound loud in his ears despite the murmuring of the crowd and the buzz of music filtering through the speakers. His gaze darted up again, examining her from head to toe, looking for a sign—or maybe an excuse—for him to show up and disrupt whatever she was doing. Except that would fly in the face of being a *good* wingman, which he had agreed to be for her against his better judgement.

'I see, and I guess this is you trying to make the best of it? Or is your reluctance more tied to the fact that there *is* something on this cruise ship that you *do* want, but you would prefer not to want it?' Sarah smiled when he raised his eyebrows, failing to hide the shock her words kicked loose in him.

'How did you…?'

She shrugged. 'This isn't a holiday for me; it's

my life. I spend most of my year bouncing between ships on different assignments. Which means I get to know a lot of people. Enough for me to categorise them. Doctors and other medical professionals sign up for different reasons, but if you boil them all down to their core, there are really only a handful of reasons someone works on a cruise rather than a hospital or a clinic.'

Theo opened his mouth to protest, but again shut it without giving in to the impulse to say the first words coming to him to defend himself. He'd not let himself dwell on *his* reason for being here, instead feeling far more comfortable hiding behind the excuse his sister had provided with her broken ankle. Sarah was right, though. If he really hadn't wanted to do this, he could have refused. Offered to pay the penalty in the contract himself.

Deep down, he knew his decision had been swayed by more than what he was willing to admit. Yes, doing a job with far lower stakes than what he'd been doing all his career was helping him appreciate why he'd gone into medicine in the first place. But then there was Catalina. Amelie had mentioned how her best friend was still going, and that had been when the *no* building in his throat had died.

But Theo couldn't admit that out loud. Quietly pining for a woman who'd always seen him more as a rival than a potential love interest was one thing. But deciding to come on a cruise because the aforementioned woman would be there too? That fell squarely into the territory of stalker vibes.

Sarah gave him a knowing smile. 'You don't have to tell me anything. I'm just an old medical officer who has seen this exact scenario play out in front of her more times than she can count.' She turned around, following his gaze as it landed on Catalina. 'And I think from all I've seen over the last few days, she might appreciate you rescuing her right now.'

He tensed at her words, focusing on Catalina's body language while trying not to get distracted by what simply *looking* at her did to him.

'I can't force myself into a situation simply because I don't like seeing it,' he said, the words an assurance to himself as much as to Sarah.

But the woman shrugged as if he hadn't laid out some solid reasoning. 'The face she's making—that's not someone who is enjoying themselves right now. And I know what her expression looks like when she *is* with someone she likes,' Sarah said with another shrug. 'But don't listen to me if you disagree. I hardly know you two, after all.'

What was he doing, standing by while Catalina tried to find someone else when *he* was right here? When he wanted this? *Her*. Sure, the hundreds of reasons why they didn't make any sense together stood right in front of him like a mountain. For one, his life was in complete disarray, and coming here on the cruise had been like hitting the pause button on that. The moment he got back to the States, it would all come back like a tidal wave. Sorting through the fallout with his parents—figuring out what *he* wanted rather than what they expected from him—would require time and space. Neither of those things would be fair in a new relationship.

Plus, she had her residency ahead of her. Theo wasn't sure if she'd applied anywhere, but with how he'd left things with his parents, he wouldn't be surprised if they'd blacklisted him across all prestigious institutions. Association with him would only hurt her chances of getting a good placement. He couldn't let that happen to her.

But what if it wasn't a relationship? From what Catalina had told him, she was looking to reclaim her life by pursuing things that brought her pleasure rather than trying to be the most impressive person in the room. Could that be what he had to offer her? A safe space to explore, confined to the duration of their trip?

'I have to go,' Theo said, pushing himself upright before he could talk himself out of it. 'Thanks for the chat,' he added as he passed by Sarah, giving her a small smile before weaving through the crowd to get to the bar.

Was she just not into men? It was the only thing Catalina could think of to explain the complete lack of chemistry she'd experienced with every single person since embarking on this cruise adventure. Surely they couldn't all be trash like Dave?

To be fair to the men who'd approached her, none of them had sunk to Dave levels of creepiness, but neither were they conjuring butterflies in her stomach, to the point where she was seriously questioning her sexuality. Had she *really* never been attracted to a man before? No, that couldn't be right.

She knew what she wanted and also what she expected. It was the swooping stomach, the bursts of electricity shooting through her entire body as Theo's lips pressed down on her—

Oops.

A flush crept up her neck, temporarily rendering her incapable of hearing anything. Not that it mattered because Brian over here wasn't getting an invitation back to her cabin. Especially not now that she'd asked Theo to move back in. He'd gone to fetch his things as soon as they'd got back from Dubrovnik, and to avoid seeing him after that almost-*whatever* at the lookout point, she'd gone straight for one of the ship's bars, intent on turning her virginity mission into reality.

Okay, so there was *one* man to whom she was attracted. Progress, right? At the very least, she could now confirm she was *capable* of attraction to the opposite sex. Just not the Brians and Daves of this ship. No, she needed to find a Theo-type person who wasn't Theo himself.

A part of her had briefly considered the possibility of going down that path with him. She'd told him everything, including her reasons. A man of his age and calibre would have more than enough experience to guide her through this.

And perhaps most importantly, one look from him was enough to turn her into a puddle. Had been for years now. Maybe that was what was happening between them. With the impromptu kiss and their renewed closeness from earlier, there was clearly something between them. For the longest time she'd thought her crush was unrequited, and she'd lived quite peacefully with that fact.

'You said you are part of the crew?' Brian asked, voice hoarse enough to scratch her ear canal. Yeah, there was no way this was going to happen tonight. Catalina had struck out once again—was that the right use of the sports metaphor?—and she would be going back alone.

Mostly alone. Were it not for her old/new roommate, who would no doubt be waiting for her.

'Yeah, I'm a doctor,' she said, her eyes roaming around the room to plot her escape route. After the encounter with Dave, at least she was getting better at that. 'And I actually have an early shift tomorrow. You know, saving lives and whatever.

One alcohol poisoning at a time. It was nice to meet you.'

She plastered on a smile and, before Brian could react, she moved away and into the crowd, ready to slink back to her cabin and lick her wounds. With every day that passed, her hopes of accomplishing her goal sank lower. Who would have thought that a virgin wouldn't just be shy about sex but also about all the preamble that led to it? The thought of suffering these conversations long enough to get to a point where she would let any of these guys near her exhausted her.

Or maybe *one* specific man had ruined her, since all this didn't apply to him. No, conversations with Theo were easy. So were the silences. And the moments in between, when they weren't really doing anything but still hanging out. Hell, even in Dubrovnik, after the world's most awkward encounter the night before, the moment they'd found each other again, it just worked. The tension had ebbed away within seconds as they'd found their rhythm again, and then it had been as if they'd never accidentally made out.

Why were things so *natural* with him, but other men were downright excruciating?

As she reached the edge of the room, a hand closed around her arm—stopping her in her tracks. Catalina whirled around, ready to tell Brian what she *really* thought of him. But the words died in her throat when she stared into the grey eyes of Theo, the sight instantly familiar and putting her at ease.

Though that lasted for a mere second before she saw the fire ablaze in his stare. Somehow the flame jumped the space between them, building up beneath her skin until her own body temperature spiked to an infernal level. She swallowed, her throat dry from the alcohol and the shouted conversation of the evening.

Theo towered over her, and when he took another step towards her she had to tip her head backwards so she could still see him. Her back pressed against the floor-to-ceiling windowpane behind her, the glass doing precious little to cool her down.

'I don't think I can be your wingman any more,' he said as he bent down next to her ear so she could hear him without shouting. His voice was low and filled with gravel, sending a shiver down her spine.

'If you were doing your wingman job today, then I have to agree. Not your best performance, seeing I'm once again solo,' she replied, though why they were taking the conversation in that direction, she wasn't sure. Nothing about his body language—or how close he stood—gave her any specific indication.

'You said I should stay away. That I frighten the men you're trying to court. So I stayed away, even though I hated sitting over there being forced to watch you pursue *other* men.' There was an edge to his voice that shot right through Catalina, settling in a swirling vortex in the pit of her stomach. What he was saying wasn't hot. It wasn't even cute. Why was she reacting as if it was?

'I'm not forcing you to watch anything,' she hissed, though the thought of him standing somewhere in the crowd and watching her did something funny to her insides. Twisted and shook them until they were completely rearranged. 'Maybe you should work on yourself before you come here on your high horse, lecturing me.'

'I promised you I would help. That doesn't just go away because I can't keep a lid on my jealousy.' His words turned into a growl—or at least that was the only word Catalina could come up with that fitted.

But her mind latched onto something else. 'Jealousy?'

His huffed laugh was warm against her cheek. 'What? You think I'm unaffected by all this? That I just kiss you one day and forget about everything the next? You are vastly overestimating my compartmentalisation skills.'

He paused, and when he breathed in his chest expanded enough for their upper bodies to touch. Her knees grew weak, and her hands—developing a will of their own—came down on either side of his collar, hanging onto him. A tremble went through Theo at the light touch. Or maybe she was the one trembling; she wasn't sure.

'Cat—' her name somehow echoed through the tiny space between them '—don't make me watch from the sidelines again. I don't think I can.' His head dipped lower, his nose pressing against the side of her throat so she could feel every exhale dance over her skin. Her grip on him tightened, fingers fisting into the fabric of his shirt.

'I'm not making you do anything,' she repeated, though keeping track of the conversation was becoming harder by the second, her brain filled with this lusty haze only *his* touch could conjure within her. Was that even possible? Could someone simply be attracted to one person and only them?

'You're not. But you're still the one who holds the solution to my dilemma.' His mouth trailed down her neck, each kiss sending renewed shivers through her until she was nothing more than a trembling mess.

'What dilemma?' Deep down, Catalina knew his struggle because she was experiencing the same one whenever she went out to find someone who would never live up to the comparison to Theo. Would never hit the same nerve or hold her attention the same way. It had been going on for years, her nurturing a one-sided crush, which had now turned out to be far less unrequited.

Only she didn't know what it meant for her—for them.

'Every person I watch you with, every time I see you laugh or smile or even touch someone's arm in a friendly way, something jolts through me and I think: this should be me.' His breath was hot against her neck, raising the hairs all the way down her arms. 'Let it be me.'

His voice was low and pleading in a way she'd never heard from Theo. It sent a thrill through her, knowing how he'd considered her. In a way that wasn't derision or cold calculation. No, he *wanted* her, the way she wanted him. Had that always been the case?

'What about…your family? Your life outside of this ship?'

Her conversation with Amelie flashed through her mind. Even though her best friend had told Theo to stay away, Catalina knew that had been a pretext. Though what exactly the younger Morgan sibling was planning was beyond her. Only that it could be nothing good.

Theo hummed, the vibration ghosting over her skin and making her arch her back to get closer to him. His lips brushed over her collarbone, and she gasped when his tongue found the hollow of her throat.

Then he straightened, touching their foreheads against each other. There was nothing but fire in his eyes. 'You're looking to break out of this pattern you're in. Choose yourself, you said? I can do that right here, within the confines of this cruise. And after it's over, we go back to our separate lives.'

A pinprick of worry broke through the tidal wave of lust crashing through her at his words. Catalina hadn't put much thought into the after. Or into the future in general. There was the matter of continuing her education as a doctor, but when she and Amelie had made the plan for the cruise they'd both promised not to think about anything else.

So Theo didn't want a relationship. That made sense. Catalina didn't want a relationship either, right? That hadn't been the goal of this entire endeavour. No, coming here had been a radical act of self-love, letting herself experience new things and leave the humdrum of her daily life behind for a bit. Gain some distance to understand who she wanted to be in the future—in her personal and professional life.

And yes, there was also the bit about her sexuality and figuring out what she liked there—in a no-strings-attached and emotionally safe way. No room to overthink things or get stuck in the same pattern of people-pleasing she had barely broken out of with her parents.

'Okay.' She breathed the word out. Through the noise of the bar, she thought he hadn't heard her when he kept staring at her, blinking almost in time with the bass vibrating through the dance floor.

But then his mouth crashed down on hers, tongue swiping over her lips and into her mouth in a greedy kiss that stole all the air from her lungs.

CHAPTER NINE

Day Ten, at sea

THEY'D BARELY MADE it through the door when Theo pounced on her. Caging her body with his, the way he had back at the bar, he pushed her against the closed door of her cabin and drew her into a lingering kiss. His hands found her hips, thumb tracing a lazy upward spiral across the fabric of her dress, kneading the spot he'd already learned was hypersensitive. Catalina caught herself half-laughing, half-moaning as the world began to contract—there was only this cubic metre of space, the twin heartbeats thudding in her ears. There was no more space for overthinking or wondering about the consequences. Theo's words had been clear. They would treat this like people treated Las Vegas: what happened on the ship, stayed on the ship.

Theo's grip tightened around her as she moaned, and the contrast between their first kiss and now was so stark it sent sparks shooting across her body. There was nothing gentle in how he held her, the hunger coiled in his fingertips, the press of his chest pinning her so tightly that every shallow breath was inhaled from him. He kissed her as if he'd been planning this for years—and for a broken fragment of a second, Catalina let herself believe he had. That this wasn't a result of circumstances but that he'd been quietly pining for her the way she had for him—hiding his true feelings behind derision.

She knew this was a dangerous path to walk down but, caught up in the moment, she couldn't stop herself.

Her hands slid under his shirt, desperate for skin and certainty. He growled, a sound that vibrated against her lips and down her spine, and then he broke the kiss just long enough to look her in the eyes. 'Stop me if you want to,' he said, voice unsteady but true.

She shook her head, incapable of words. If anything, the pressure of his restraint—the tension in his jaw, how much he was obviously holding back—made her want him more. She wanted him unspooled and raw, not the carefully presented version of Theo Morgan the world saw.

He dropped his head to her throat, mouthing kisses across her collarbone while his hands mapped her body as if he were learning it in Braille. She gasped, legs turning to water as her back arched, every gentle scrape of his stubble drawing a soft moan from her.

'I never want you to stop,' Catalina replied, unable to keep the truth of her feelings hidden. Not when they were so close, his breath mingling with hers and his hands touching her skin reverently. Delicately. As if he wanted her for more than just this moment.

Theo responded with nothing more than a growl, and his hands slipped to the hem of her dress, fingers toying with it while he pressed his face into her neck. She tipped her chin, hungry for more, but he bunched the fabric of her dress and palmed her hips, steering her from the door to the bed with stumbling steps. They crashed onto the narrow mattress and she caught herself with a laugh, the sound melting into another gasp as he pressed her down, hands bracketing her ribs, kissing her as if he could swallow the sound of her moans to keep them forever.

'You really thought we could sleep on this bed together for the rest of this cruise without anything happening?' he asked as he pushed himself up on his elbows to look down at her. He settled in the cradle of her parted thighs, and when she felt his arousal press against her this time Catalina braced herself for the same panic to sweep through her.

It didn't come. No, she stayed wrapped in the luscious fog of passion, her mind not drifting to the thought of her virginity, of the consequences that might await them if they did this. Tomorrow seemed too far away to consider when she was burning up inside.

Theo *wanted* her. It was as clear as it could get. Undeniable, yet her mind still grappled with the idea. How long had this been going on right in front of her eyes? Had Theo always been interested, and somehow she'd not connected the dots? Was this the reason for their antagonistic relationship? She tried to remember who had started the sniping between them all those years ago, but she couldn't. Not when Theo's hands found their way under her dress again, callused palms scraping up her bare thighs until he got to her stomach.

His breathing hitched. She felt it; the tremor travelling down the line of his forearm as he raked his knuckles up her side. 'I'm going to lose my mind,' he muttered, half to himself and half to her, before ducking down to mouth along her jaw. There was reverence in the hunger, every kiss and squeeze a question—*Are you sure? Do you want this?*—that kept repeating until she wanted to sob *Yes, yes, yes* into the hot space between their bodies.

She found herself greedy for every new sensation: the velvet heat of his tongue at her ear, the pressure of him nudging her thighs further apart, the way he seemed desperate to touch all of her at once.

'Cat,' he said, voice raw.

She opened her eyes—when had she shut them?—and the pure need in his gaze sent her head spinning. But beneath it was something more. A glimmer of concern? When she realised it, Catalina almost burst out laughing. Of course he would worry about her—about taking advantage of her?—even when it was clear as day she wanted him. Had wanted him for far longer than she was willing to admit. Even though she'd tried her best to fulfil her mission and reclaim control of her life, none of the men she'd met had been even remotely interesting to her. Only Theo had caught her attention in every way she needed.

Theo's lips hovered just above hers, his weight braced on trembling arms. For a moment, he seemed on the verge of pulling back, the old reticence fighting with the heat in his gaze. Catalina reached, curling her fingers into his hair. She pulled him close enough that his breath fanned her lips, close enough she could taste the doubt, the want, the worry.

'I want this,' she whispered. 'I want you.' The words bubbled out, unpractised and rough, a confession more than a command.

But it worked as the latter. Theo's mouth crashed onto hers, bruising and needy. Catalina arched up against him, fingers tunnelling beneath the collar of his shirt, frantic to feel the heat of his skin. She clawed at the buttons, popping the first two before he even registered her intent. A helpless, strangled sound broke in his throat as she yanked his shirt from his waistband, hands spreading over the hard terrain of his chest. He tensed beneath her touch, every muscle drawn taut, then seemed to melt at the sweep of her palm up and over his heart.

Catalina let out a moan when Theo pressed closer, her hands skimming across his skin. Was this what it felt like to touch someone else? As if there was a low current running beneath their skin, making electricity jump back and forth between them.

'Do you like touching me?' he asked.

She blinked, startled by the vulnerability in it. As if he worried the answer could be anything else but the one she gave.

'Yes,' she said, and her palms pressed harder, as if to demonstrate.

His smile was slow but radiant, forcing the breath out of her lungs. 'Good. I want you to enjoy every touch. Make sure you're ready. And if things are going too fast, let me know.'

Theo didn't wait for her reply. His hands tightened around her hips and then he flipped her around, face first into the cushions. Fabric rustled above her—no doubt the shirt she'd only bothered to half remove—and then his fingers brushed over the nape of her neck. It was enough to send another wave of heat through her, tiny fires following as Theo opened her zip all the way down to her spine.

He splayed his hand over her skin, fingers fanning out and touching both of her shoulder blades. In her peripheral vision, she could see him move his other hand to peel the dress away from her body. Then he bent over, his hand vanishing—replaced by his face. His mouth, more specifically, lavishing her heated skin with more feather-light kisses. She gasped when his tongue darted out, licking her in a place she'd never thought to be particularly sensitive.

But then again, what did she know about sex? A half-drunk make-out session with some guy she couldn't remember was as far as her physical experience went. Not really something she could call *adventurous* by any means. No, as far as exploration was concerned, falling onto a far too soft mattress in a tiny cabin on a floating hunk of steel with her best friend's brother was the most adventurous Catalina had got in, well, ever.

And yes, having it all laid out like that, she might be in *a bit* of trouble. Was this actually the worst idea she'd ever had?

But before her thoughts could stray too far from the present moment, Theo reached the base of her spine and placed an open-mouthed kiss there. Even though her skin was heated all over, his breath still scorched her when he let out a stuttering breath that gave her an idea of how much this affected him, too.

This was the thought she kept coming back to. The idea that almost turned incomprehensible if she thought about it too long. No one had ever *wanted* her, at least not in the form she came. Hadn't she spent years struggling to be recognised by her family, until she'd simply given up on trying?

'Will you get on your knees for me, Cat?' Theo's words were a hushed whisper, his hands skating up her thighs and pushing up the fabric of her dress until it was bunched around her waist.

He lifted her up when she moved her already rubbery limbs, helping her get off the mattress enough so he could peel the dress away from her entirely. But instead of putting her back down on the bed, Theo pulled her towards him until her back was flush against his front. His arms snaked around her, caressing her stomach before tracing lazy circles upwards until he reached the underside of her breasts.

'You're not wearing a bra,' he whispered next to her ear before placing a kiss below it. Catalina wanted to respond, but her words turned into a moan when he palmed both of her breasts.

'The advantage of having small boobs,' she breathed out between pants, losing most of her faculty to speak when his thumbs brushed along her nipples.

'Am I completely vain for wanting to believe you did this for me? You knew how I would react to seeing you walk around in this dress, looking at everyone but me?' He growled the words, punctuating every pause with another kiss or lick to her neck while his hands lavished her with the attention she'd known she'd wanted but hadn't realised just *how good* it would feel.

She had thought about Theo when deciding what to wear, though even now, in the position they were in, there was no way she could admit that. They might be naked in front of each other, but there were still some boundaries, right? And admitting how hot this jealous act of his was getting her—and how unnecessary it was for him to compare himself to anyone in her eyes—crossed a line. Their dynamic was already shaky, and she was under no illusions that this wouldn't change it further.

But right now, Catalina didn't care. She'd come here with a goal, and the only person capable of getting her to this point seemed to be Theo.

'If I say yes, will you touch me?' she said instead, head lolling back onto his shoulder when he squeezed her nipple hard enough to bring her to the edge of pleasure and pain.

He didn't answer. Instead, he moved his hand downward, playing with the seam of her underwear for a few excruciating seconds before dipping below the fabric. 'You tell me what feels good, okay?'

She meant to tease him, to say something snarky, but the moment his fingers slid over and inside her—one, then two, with a slow and deliberate push—words simply vanished from her mind. He curled them as he pumped in and out, drawing a sound from her chest she'd never made before, a whimper that seemed to please him as much as it shocked herself. Theo's chin pressed to her shoulder, his mouth collecting every gasp and *'yes'* as he worked her with slow strokes and caresses, learning every twitch and spasm and shiver like a language only they spoke.

Her limbs and muscles stopped working altogether as the pressure at her core built, but his other hand wrapped around her waist, bracing her. Holding her up, holding her together. The world shrank to the slick, rhythmic pressure of his touch, and the only thing she could manage was to press her hips back, greedy for more friction, more of him. When he added his thumb, circling tight and insistent, the pleasure became a throttle, making her collapse back into his chest with a hoarse, shuddering exhale.

Theo's mouth worked up her neck, nipping and sucking at the tender skin below her ear as his fingers coaxed her higher. 'That's it, Cat,' he murmured, voice dark and raw. 'Let yourself go. Don't hold back.'

She didn't. She couldn't. Not when her knees were buckling and her hands scrabbled for purchase against the wall, not when every expert curl and stroke set her aflame.

Her climax took her by surprise, erupting from the depths of her core and radiating outwards like a shot of liquid sun. She locked up for a moment, then splintered, gasping out his name so loud she thought it might echo through the bulkhead. Theo steadied her, hands unyielding and gentle all at once.

For a suspended moment, neither of them moved, the air thick with something elemental that had never existed between them before. Eventually, he eased her back onto the bed, settling her gently and smoothing a damp strand of hair from her brow.

'You good?' he asked.

Catalina rolled over onto her back, blinking up at the ceiling, vision blurring at the white swirl of cheap cabin paint. She felt emptied out and refilled in equal measure.

'I'm—' Her voice faltered, threaded through with laughter. 'Yeah. I think I'm better than good.'

Theo came up to drag her into another kiss, layered with the want she could feel radiating from herself. There was a subdued franticness to it, and it was enough to stoke the cooling embers back into frenzy.

'I'm glad,' he said between kisses, his weight

settling against her—somehow already familiar. 'Do you still want to continue?'

Would any other person have been this careful with her? This reassuring and checking in at every turn? Catalina couldn't imagine it. Then again, her entire mission had been about simply getting it done. Striking it off the list so she could move on with her life. Shed the final vestiges that were holding her back and mould a version of her life she wanted to live in. Not the version she'd chosen for her parents' sake. Not the one she thought her ambition dictated.

Was it odd that, looking up into Theo's passion-glazed eyes, she could see that future, despite not really having thought about it?

She nodded, and when he still hesitated, Catalina wrapped her legs around his waist and pulled him closer until his length pressed against her through the fabric of his trousers.

'Are *you* sure?' she asked, letting her body guide her into what felt good as she ground against him. His low hiss at the continued touch sent a thrill through her.

'I've never been unsure about wanting you, Cat. Ever.'

Catalina writhed against him, the intimate form of her name doing something to shut down her brain. There were only two ways she'd ever heard him call her 'Cat'. As a warning had been the top contender. But now—pure want. It was the better version.

'Then do this with me. Let's just…do what we want for the first time in our lives instead of what is expected of us.' She reached out to cup his cheek as she spoke, her fingers trailing along his jawbone. Theo turned his head to the side, and Catalina shivered when he pressed a gentle kiss at the centre of her palm.

'Okay,' was all he said. Then he shifted onto his knees before getting off the bed entirely. His sudden absence was disorienting, and for a panicked second she thought she'd said the wrong thing. But then Theo reached for his belt, unbuckling it with a clink of metal before it joined the heap of clothes on the floor. Catalina's gaze dropped to his hands, watching him as he undid the button on his trousers and then pushed them down. Stepping out of them brought him closer to the bed again, and even in the dim light filtering through the window she could see the impression of his manhood through the fabric of his underwear.

'Cat.' He repeated her name, and her head whipped up. 'Since you've been planning this, do you have protection?'

Why did the words make her blush? She was a doctor, for goodness' sake. Of course she had prepared. In fact, she had prepared maybe a bit too well by buying different sizes and types. If any customs agent had looked at the luggage from her flight they probably had a very different idea of who she was as a person.

And now she was about to show Theo the pile of condoms she'd brought with her. Oh God. In all of her weirdly analytical fantasies of losing her virginity, that hadn't been a problem because, well, Theo was nowhere near them.

Whether her temporary dismay was obvious or Theo was simply that good at reading her, she wasn't sure. His mouth softened into a smile as he asked, 'Did you overprepare for this occasion and now you don't know what to offer me?'

Catalina couldn't help but laugh. He knew her that well, didn't he?

'I may have,' she hedged, even though there was no reason to, but their ingrained dynamic was hard to shake. Also, something about the familiarity put her at ease.

Taking a breath, she nodded towards a tote bag hanging from a hook. Theo turned around, and she couldn't stop her eyes from taking him in from head to toe as he reached over and took the bag. The cardboard boxes knocked against each other as he rifled through them, and when his hand disappeared again, he held up a box.

'You really had big plans for this cruise,' he said as he came back, opening the box and fishing out one of the foil-wrapped condoms. Then—faster than Catalina could process—Theo hooked his thumbs along his waistband and pulled his underwear down. The condom came next, rolling on in one smooth motion.

The heat in her cheeks renewed. 'Shut up. There were twenty types, all promising different things. How was I supposed to know which one to bring? I didn't know there were so many types of penises.'

Theo cocked his head to the side, his lips widening in a grin. 'You're a doctor, Cat.'

'Yeah, a general medicine doctor.'

'The male anatomy is covered in there.'

Catalina pouted. 'Just…shut up and come over here before you ruin the mood.'

She knew as she said it that this wasn't the sort of challenge she should throw at Theo. The grin turned into a smirk.

'My mood has never been better.'

'Ugh, where is the Theo that was all worried about this?'

She should have expected the teasing. The heat of the moment had distracted them both, though it wasn't like their need for each other was diminishing. No, the tension remained thick between them.

Theo's eyes slipped down her body when she pressed her thighs together in search of some friction, and the smirk slipped for a second—giving her just the idea she needed. If he was going to drag this out just for his own amusement, she would see how tough his restraint really was.

She brought one of her hands up to her chest, palming her breast and flicking her thumb over her nipple. Her gasp turned into a laugh when his eyes darted up, smirk wiped off his face.

'What are you—?'

His words trailed off when Catalina moved her other hand down over her stomach and between her legs, where she stroked herself just the way he had a few moments ago. She watched him with delicious intent, waiting for him to make his move as she pleasured herself. Theo's eyes flared, pupils blown wide. He stood frozen for a few moments, then he was on her, replacing her hand with his. His mouth crashed down on hers and swallowed the building moans and just as Catalina thought she was ready to flow away into the clouds again, she felt him between her legs.

Pressure built in a way both strange and deeply familiar, and she let out a gasp when he pressed into her, slow and careful. The burn was exquisite and foreign, a tight, bright flash of sensation that made her hips buck and her hands fist in the sheets.

Theo stilled, holding absolutely silent. 'This okay?' he asked, his mouth brushing the damp wisps of hair at her temple.

It took her longer than expected to find her voice. 'Yeah—just...keep going.'

He nodded once, the movement sharp with restraint. He thrust again, a little deeper this time, his gaze never leaving her face. It was almost too much—the intensity behind those eyes, the feeling of being opened and taken, but also the way he seemed to want to memorise every millisecond. Catalina squeezed her legs tighter around him, needing the extra pressure, and he hissed out a soft expletive that made her laugh. How often had she seen him lose his composure like that? Never.

She wanted to tease him for how serious he looked, but then Theo started to move in earnest, and it was like nothing else had ever mattered. The rhythm built between them, slow and relentless, and he was so precisely attuned to her she lost track of her own body, just feeling and being felt. His hands covered hers, fingers interlocked. Every movement tugged a new sound from her until she was making noises she'd never heard before.

'God, Cat,' he breathed into her neck. 'You're incredible.'

She wanted to laugh, to dismiss or deflect, but there was nothing left in her to argue. Just the heat of him, the way every thrust felt like it fused them closer together—sealing a bond that had been in existence since the day they'd met.

She didn't know exactly when the second climax started, only that it was an avalanche from her core—an aftershock that rippled through her legs and pulled an answering groan from Theo. He slammed in harder, dragged out, and her world snapped to a pinhole of white, her body clenching hard and then shattering in a way that was so raw and so good she thought she might dissolve right there between the sheets.

Reduced to nothing but the sensations running through her body, she cried out his name and felt him stiffen around her.

Theo lost all composure then, the carefulness replaced by something wild. He pushed in once, twice, and then let out a hoarse cry. Their bodies kept pressing against each other, sweat-slicked and trembling—boneless. For a long, suspended second, nothing existed but the hiss of their mingled breath and the thump of blood in her own ears.

Finally, Theo slumped gently to one side, rolling to face her so their bodies stayed entwined. He cradled her cheek, tracing her jaw with a thumb, blinking as if sight itself was a new sensation. Neither of them spoke for a while. They were both too spent, too stunned, too raw for words. But the silence wasn't awkward.

It felt as if something long lurking between them had been fused together and made whole by the fire of their passion.

CHAPTER TEN

Day Fourteen, Florence

SOMEHOW, THE CRUISE had turned out so much different from what Theo had anticipated. Sure, his expectations had been low to begin with since he wasn't really a person known to 'have fun' easily. And a part of him still suspected his sister had somehow orchestrated this. Though breaking her own ankle to push him in this direction seemed extreme even for Amelie.

Then again, they were Morgans. She might have rejected the family dynasty, but that didn't make her less tenacious than the rest of the family. She simply channelled those feelings to her advantage. Unlike Theo, who had spent far too much time doing exactly as he was told.

At least that had changed on the cruise, for better or for worse. The old Theo—the Theo from before, who hadn't failed miserably at the one thing he was supposed to be good at—wouldn't have given in to a jealous impulse and gone back to Catalina's cabin. The old Theo would have missed out.

'Have you been to Italy before?' Catalina asked next to him, arm slung through his and pulling him closer into her with every other step.

He chuckled, looking down at where her hand rested on his bicep. It was an oddly comforting gesture. Not just her holding him but all the other brief moments they'd shared in the last few days—ever since they'd slept together. 'You seem to be under the impression I've led an incredibly adventurous life, when nothing could be further from the truth. When do you think I had the time to travel the world?'

Catalina shrugged, a smile dancing on her lips. 'I don't know. After you finished up med school, you must have gone somewhere. Don't important people travel around for conferences and consultation and all that stuff?'

Not in the field of emergency medicine, he wanted to say. But instcad, what came out was, 'You think I'm important people?'

Her hand tightened around his upper arm in an affectionate squeeze. 'You are to me.'

She had said things like that before, off-handedly. Always at the end of a conversation and never with enough intention for Theo to dig further.

But the words stuck with him, slow-release, winding through the soft, unremarkable Sunday morning in Florence. They strolled along the bank of the Arno River, the air sharp with salt and rosemary from the row of restaurants across the water. Couples and families drifted by, unconcerned by the heaviness slowly building in Theo's chest.

He waited for the anxiety to fade, but it stitched itself tighter with each step. He searched for the right moment to bring it up, to ask Catalina what she thought would happen after this. After the cruise, the ship, the bubble. In a week they'd return to port, and she'd be off to find her residency, and he—what was he now? A man who'd burned all his bridges except the one they both stood on together for as long as the steel hull surrounded them.

He tried to picture her in Chicago, doing rounds, laughing with the other residents over takeout. He tried to picture himself still in New York City, calling her after a shift, making plans, fighting for a corner of her life she'd already spent so long defending from the world. Would she want that? Could he even do it, after years of keeping everyone—especially *her*—at arm's length? Did he even know how to let her in?

Catalina stopped short, shifting her weight so abruptly he nearly walked into her. She'd spotted something on the other side of the street—some architectural curiosity, a lintel carved with cherubs, nothing that would have caught his eye. She snapped a photo with her phone, then glanced at him with a bright smile that showed him far more of the future than he wanted to admit.

If he were a different man, maybe he could find a way to keep her. But it would be too selfish, dragging her into the world he'd burned to the ground around himself.

'I love this place. Similar to Sicily but somehow completely different. Do you know what I mean?' Catalina looked around, her skirt billowing as she whirled, and her eyes sparkled when they landed back on him. 'No wonder this is one of the top honeymoon destinations. It's so romantic.'

The smile on her lips froze. Or maybe it was his lips feeling less flexible than usual. Her words sank into the silence between them. Catalina's eyes widened a fraction before she said, 'Platonic, I mean! It's all super *platonic* here.' Then she spun around and stalked on ahead, taking pictures now and then without actually looking at her phone.

Her awkward giggle was almost enough to make him laugh if a version of this moment hadn't happened every day since their night together. They hadn't slowed down that night—or any night since—though the next morning they hadn't spoken about what it meant. They couldn't get entangled with each other beyond this trip, and Theo needed them both to remember that.

No, that wasn't true or fair. He needed to remind *himself* of that far more than Catalina. Because the moment he'd felt her around him, under him, something formless inside him had solidified. The way he'd felt about her since they'd first met finally blossoming into something he'd known had been there all along: affection.

Love.

Theo was so gone for Catalina—had been for a pathetically long span of his adulthood—that the kiss they'd shared had been enough to tip him over the edge.

He could no longer deny his feelings and how they had been brewing inside him. Or how kissing her—sleeping with her—had changed everything for him.

He was in love with her, and he could do nothing about it. Couldn't change what was inside him, but neither could he accept it. It wouldn't be fair to her. Catalina was starting her medical career, choosing a specialty that would determine the rest of her life. There were few more important decisions in the life of a career physician, and Theo would not stand in the way of that. Would not let her attach her name to his, even romantically, when he had tarnished his career and his name beyond repair.

He just needed to figure out how to walk away from her without breaking.

Romantic. The word echoed through Catalina's head for the duration of their visit in Florence. Theo hadn't responded—even when she'd gone on to make it worse by saying she thought Italy was super *platonic*.

At the time it had felt like a good save, but she had to admit now, her brain had gone into a weird survival mode she hadn't intended.

Things had been quietly tense between them since then. Or maybe it was all in her head; Catalina wasn't entirely sure. Because he hadn't sought to distance himself after that. She'd made sure he had plenty of opportunity at every stop they'd made in Florence. Now she stood at the sink of the cabin—*their* cabin—brushing her teeth while Theo sat on the bed with a book in his hand.

She looked at him through the mirror, her chest squeezing tight. Despite knowing this should be casual and that reacting any other way would be misguided, Catalina couldn't stop her brain from latching on to the mundanity of what she was seeing—and how much she craved it. How much she *wanted* to stand at a sink every night and see Theo sitting on a bed. Her bed. Their bed?

There was nothing sexual about this moment, and that was the worrying part. The thing between them was supposed to be *only* that. Heat and sweat and slick skin against each other. Not… this. Not quiet moments in the evening, not living side by side as if it was the most natural thing in the world.

'So, what's your plan after this?' she asked as

her thoughts veered into a direction she didn't want them to take.

Theo looked up from the book, and something flickered over his features—shock? It had gone too soon for her to catch, but her heart lurched anyway. Were they not supposed to speak about *afterwards*? Was that somehow also indicative of her growing feelings for him, like using the word *romantic*?

Or telling him he was important to her?

Theo looked back down at the book. Stared at it long enough that Catalina thought he might have decided not to answer her question.

Fair enough. Why should he answer? Asking questions like that about each other was more than they had agreed on, after all. It wasn't as if she'd spoken about these things before with him. Why should she ask now? Nothing had changed between them, other than she'd finally lost her virginity, putting her own happiness first after years of denying it.

Putting her heart on the line for a man who'd told her—shown her—over and over again that he wasn't interested in her like that.

'I don't know. To be honest, I've so far avoided thinking about the *after* because I have no idea what to do.' The words were so quiet that for a moment she thought she'd imagined them. But when she looked up at the mirror and at his reflection again, his eyes were on her.

Putting down the toothbrush, she turned towards him. And then she asked the question that had been on her mind since even before they had come on this cruise together.

'What happened to you?'

Theo had hinted at things here and there, granting her tiny glimpses into a still deeply hurtful episode in his life. But he had yet to share any details. A part of Catalina didn't want to pry. Mainly because it wasn't her place to know him like that, right? As they had discussed, this was a casual arrangement and he was helping her out. None of this was supposed to mean anything, and she would be damned if she was the one to suddenly change their arrangement.

Wouldn't that be what he would expect from her? The virgin falling in love with her first lover?

Except maybe it was already too late for that.

'I crashed out.' Three words and nothing else. Yet Catalina's heart stopped when she heard them. Turning around, she stepped out of the tiny bathroom and leant against the doorframe while looking at him.

'I don't even know how it happened. The work had always been stressful, but something on that day just snapped in me. I realised I could spend my entire life chasing this idea—this legacy—and still never succeed.'

Catalina's grip on the doorframe tightened as his words echoed within her, finding a vulnerable place within her. She knew the meaning behind them, even though she didn't know what it felt like to be him. But she too had chased something she would never reach. Was standing right here because she'd had enough. Didn't want to centre her self-worth on the approval of others.

Theo shook his head, letting out a mirthless laugh. 'One day I woke up and I realised I didn't want any of this. Have never wanted to be a Morgan but was pushed into it my entire life. I realised that the reason my chest feels tight when I see my sister calling is because she reminds me of what I could have been. If only I were braver. But instead of being an adult about it, I burned it all to the ground. Left the hospital and my family with no notice. Just turned my back and walked out.'

His voice grew more monotone as he went on until he sounded as if he were far away. It broke something inside Catalina seeing him like this. Before she could decide if her action was appropriate in their not quite friends with benefits arrangement, she stepped forward and pulled the book out of his hands. Then she took them and put them around her waist while pulling him closer towards her.

Her fingers tunnelled through his hair, pressing his head against her stomach in an embrace that was somehow more intimate than what they'd been doing.

'Don't be so hard on yourself. You were thrust

into a position you didn't want because of family obligations. I don't know what you went through, but I know the stories about your parents. Know what Amelie went through herself.'

The Morgan parents had earned a reputation for being ruthless; Catalina knew that much. They'd been less than enthusiastic to learn their daughter would rather do her internship at the same hospital as her best friend than a Morgan-approved hospital. They'd never been overtly negative towards Catalina, but she'd wondered at times if they blamed her for Amelie's decision to carve her own path.

'I was raised to be exactly like this. From early on, I knew what was expected of me and what my future would look like. I knew it would be a long and hard road, but also that I'm lucky to be in this position. Many struggle to get to where I was, and that is due in large part to my privilege.'

Catalina wanted to object, but the words caught in her throat. Hadn't she thought the same thing? Not about Theo specifically, but about how hard she'd had to work to get accepted into Attano Memorial for her internship when Amelie had simply walked in and received a space due to her name.

She finally found her voice. 'You're not your parents' expectations, Theo. You're not even the version of yourself they imagined. You're just you. That's always been enough for everyone except maybe them.' She slid her hands to either side of his face, forcing him to look at her, and the desperation in his eyes made her chest hurt. 'You don't have to be the best. You don't have to fix everyone. You can just…be. No one who matters would be disappointed by that.'

Theo's eyes flinched from hers, a muscle jerking in his jaw as he looked away, but she felt the shift in him. She could see it, the way her words had unsettled his foundation. For a moment, he looked almost offended at the suggestion. As if she couldn't possibly know what she was talking about, when she might in fact be the only person who understood what he was saying right now.

'You don't know that,' he said, so quietly she almost missed it. 'You don't know what it's like to have this expectation hanging over your head. To have all choice removed from you before you even knew they were there. My parents—they didn't get to build a dynasty upon failure. What I did to them, the way I left, will have harmed their relationships. Their reputation. I won't be able to—'

'Who cares about their reputation, Theo? They will be all right, even without you.' The look in his eyes, the genuine hurt she saw there, was almost too much to bear. Was this what he'd carried around with him since leaving the hospital? 'My parents might not have built a dynasty, but they still act like I was never enough, no matter what I do or did or am. All they care about is… See, I don't even know. I just know that I spent far too much time trying to please them when I should have been living my life.'

Theo breathed out, his head drooping back down. The stubble on his cheeks scraped against her exposed stomach as he pushed his face against her. They stayed still like that, and Catalina thought the conversation was over when he said, 'How did you free yourself from that? Because I don't know who I am outside of what they expected me to be.'

Catalina's arms tightened around him, her heart breaking at the fragility in his tone. In all the years of knowing him, she'd never seen him like that. Never imagined him as someone who could get to this point. But of course he could. He was made out of flesh and blood and bones and feelings, like herself. Something that had been so easy to forget when she'd put him on a pedestal for the entire time they'd known each other.

She had thought seeing Theo come was the pinnacle of beauty. But watching him unravel like he was right now was something completely different. More profound and intimate than sex could ever be.

And it pushed her right over a cliff she knew she couldn't go over.

'You are Theodore Morgan. You are a caring older brother. A competent doctor. And the most thoughtful lover I could have asked for.' Her cheeks burned as she said that, and her heart accelerated to the point where she thought it was going to leap out of her body. But she continued on, letting the words she'd kept bottled inside her for the last few days out—even though she knew she shouldn't. Knew it went against what they'd discussed. But they needed to come out because she knew that even if he might not feel the same way, the hurt part of Theo she saw right now deserved to know that he was loved. Even if it was one-sided.

'You are worthy of whatever you put your mind to, and you are not beholden to other people's expectations. I know this even though it took me so long to see it for myself.' She paused, her voice quivering. But she couldn't let herself hesitate for too long or she wouldn't be able to say it. 'If you were standing right here where I am, looking at you through my eyes, you would see a caring, resilient man. One who was pushed to the brink by expectations far too big for anyone's shoulders. You would see a man that's loved.'

Were her words too obscure? Because if she flipped them around, they could mean something else. Of course Theo was loved—he probably knew that. Oh God, she'd never had a conversation like this with anyone ever. And here she'd thought losing her virginity would solve all of her problems, only to find herself plunged into an even deeper mess. Because she'd slept with the one man she had feelings for, and even though she'd convinced herself she wouldn't slip deeper into it, she couldn't deny the feelings fluttering alive inside her every time she looked at Theo.

The feelings that had been building since that night. No, even before that. Their first night together hadn't been the start of this but the catalyst bringing it all out of hiding.

Theo's gaze shot up to hers. Her chest squeezed so tight, the air fled her lungs. Catalina wasn't sure what she was waiting for. What she was *hoping* for. In truth, there were no plans or expectations or anything. Yet something inside her gave in when she saw his eyes shutter.

Slowly, as if he had to think through it, Theo shook his head. Kept shaking it until she wasn't sure if he was stuck with something in his ear. The silence spread, unlike any other between them. Thick and ready to cut with a knife. Tight enough to snap. Hard enough she knew it would hurt.

'Theo, I...'

'No.' The one word echoed through the tiny cabin in an unexpected acoustic phenomenon. Catalina flinched despite herself.

'Theo, I'm trying to tell—'

He didn't let her finish her sentence. 'No, you can't do that, Cat. We had—an agreement from the beginning. About what this could and couldn't be.'

'I know that.' Her voice failed her, turning frail

when she needed to be loud. Confident. Because that was the kind of man Theo was. Even if he thought he was at his lowest, he was still so much more confident and poised than she could ever imagine being. She'd struggled to make her parents proud even after years of trying. Then she had given up rather than have her spirit crushed one more time.

'I think I should take a walk,' Catalina said, her voice barely a whisper. She needed to get out of this room.

Theo jumped to his feet at her words. 'No, please… I—' He sighed, hand half outstretched towards her and hanging in midair.

'I'm sorry,' he said, his voice so hollow it barely filled the gap between them. 'I'm sorry for being like this. You deserve someone who isn't—' He cut himself off, the look in his eyes so raw she almost reached for him again, despite everything.

'I don't want someone else,' Catalina said. She wasn't sure what had possessed her to tell the truth—stubbornness, or simple exhaustion from holding back. 'I want you, Theo. Like, I thought I could keep it contained to just now. This ship. But you and I both know this has been going on far longer, and taking that step with you didn't make my feelings for you any less.'

He stared at her, and for a moment she thought he might say it, whatever was building at the back of his throat. Instead, his hands clenched, then released. 'Catalina, you have a whole future ahead of you. You're going to pick your residency, excel in your specialty, build your own name. You shouldn't be…tied to someone like me, especially after what I've done. It's not fair to you.'

She swallowed, feeling the heat in her throat, hating how every word made her want him more, not less. 'I'm not afraid of that, and I do not think you should be either. No one is going to judge me by the company I keep, Theo. I know your family is famous, but even the Morgans have limits.'

Theo shook his head, unwilling—or maybe unable—to see her point. To trust her when she said she wanted him, even if it came with its issues. Her entire life had been nothing but difficult. There was no way she couldn't handle whatever he brought with him.

'You don't— There will be consequences waiting for me back home. You don't just up and leave in my world. Not with a name like mine and the weight that comes with it. My parents will have done some damage control for their brand, and there's no doubt in my mind they did it at my expense. I wouldn't be surprised if I'm blacklisted at every major institute in the States.' Theo dropped his hand, his gaze turning sharp. 'I don't want you to wake up months from now and realise I'm holding you back. That being with me ruined your chances at important things—your career.'

Catalina could almost laugh at the irony—after

all these years, after all those late-night panic sessions with Amelie about how she was always second-best, it had turned out she'd fallen for a man who'd put himself at dead last. She wanted to kick something. She wanted, even more, to shake Theo until he admitted he was worth as much as anyone, that what he'd done was survive, not destroy.

Hell, he was so worried about her career when she didn't even know where she wanted to go. What to do.

She shook her head, arms crossed to keep herself from reaching for him. 'You won't ruin anything for me,' she said, the words hot and desperate and, honestly, a little humiliating. But Catalina didn't care. Not after all this—she'd flung herself off the edge, and she refused to hide her feelings just because he wouldn't catch her on the way down. 'I don't want to wake up in five years and wish I had been braver. I can fight my own battles, Theo. I want to choose you.'

He stared at her, his silence hammering out a new pulse in the room, until Catalina had to close her eyes. The cabin's fluorescent light suddenly felt raw, the sheets a mess on their bed. *Their bed.* If she started crying, she'd never stop. Not until they reached port, or maybe never.

She forced a laugh, brittle as dry leaves. 'God, I sound like an idiot. I know you said you didn't want anything serious, and now I'm—'

Theo cut her off, voice rough. 'You're not an

idiot, Cat. You're the only person on this planet who's ever made me want more.'

Any second now he'd start making sense, right? Because right now he wasn't, with his words contradicting each other from one breath to the next. He wanted more—wanted her? But he said no more, not giving her any indication of where they could go or what was left to do.

She made him want more. Surely that had to mean something?

'So, what? You want this. I want this. Yet we can't have it because of some arbitrary thing you invented?'

That was what it boiled down to and that was what she couldn't understand. There was nothing standing in their way. No reason why this couldn't be real. Not unless…

'Is it because of my lack of experience? You don't see yourself with someone who you have to teach stuff. It's fun for a temporary arrangement, but not something you want in your actual life.'

This had to be it. Even though it had been revelatory for Catalina, she was under no illusions that it might have been more skewed towards her pleasure than his. With someone more experienced, he probably wouldn't have to go as slow, or explain things or—only one time though—stop in the middle of it because of some discomfort.

Confined to a ship in the middle of the ocean,

maybe she was simply the easiest option. But there were others out there. Better options.

A line appeared between Theo's brows, confusion mixing with something else in his gaze. But there was no denial. Not immediately. No, he was thinking—about how to let her down easy? Or how to lie to her because he didn't want to hurt her feelings?

'Oh my God, *this* is the reason? Are you serious?' All that talk about careers and his life being in shambles, but in truth he just didn't want someone like her.

Catalina was the problem here.

'No, Cat. Now you're putting words in my mouth. I hesitate because...'

Catalina gave him two shaky breaths to get his thoughts together, but when he still looked at her without saying anything, she shook her head. 'I need to leave,' she said, though she had no idea where she'd go. They were about to leave Florence, and even if she could get off the ship, she still had responsibilities. Even though another week trapped in close proximity with Theo sounded like the worst experience on the planet.

Maybe it was her turn to sleep on the lido deck. The temperature would be warm enough. Before she could think about it for too long, Catalina began to scrabble around in the drawers, putting on whatever clothes she could find. When she was ready to leave, she found Theo standing in front of the door, pleading in his eyes.

'Catalina, you don't understand. This has nothing to do with you and everything to do with me. I'm the one who has problems—who isn't in the right space to give you what you deserve. Don't even think for a second this is about you.'

Catalina felt the air compress in the tiny cabin as she reached for the door, her hand trembling—anger or heartbreak, she couldn't tell. 'You don't get to make that decision for me,' she said, each word scraping raw against her teeth. 'If you want to finish things, fine. But don't spin it as some noble sacrifice on my behalf.'

Theo's posture stiffened. For a split second, she saw the old version of him, the one who could freeze a room with his presence alone. But it crumpled just as fast, dissolving into a slouch she'd never seen before.

'I should be the one to go. You shouldn't have to leave your own space.' The words were stiff, but there was nothing performative about the way he balled his hands into fists at his sides, as if the only thing keeping him there was sheer will.

Catalina hovered between the bed and the door with Theo blocking her way—frozen mid-step. She didn't know what she'd expected. A fight? Pleading? An explanation that didn't feel like it fell apart under the slightest scrutiny?

'Don't worry, I'll stay out of your way,' he said.

Theo shot her one look filled with the agony unfurling in her own chest, and then he pushed the door open and left. In the same way he had on that first day, only now everything was different between them. It was what Catalina had wanted, right? To be a new person at the end of this trip. Someone in charge of her mind and body, doing what she felt was right for her for the first time in her life.

She just hadn't considered that it would feel so miserable, and all because of Theodore Morgan.

Catalina took a deep breath, but when she released it, it came out in a rattle. They still had a week left on the cruise and whatever had been between them had blown up in their faces. He'd said he'd stay out of her way, but how was he going to do that? Avoiding him at work would be simple enough, but what about the cabin? The rest of the trips?

They'd have to be adults and find a solution. *But not now*, Catalina thought as she let herself fall on the messy bed.

She could think about all of the consequences later. For now, all she wanted to do was curl up into a ball and listen to the low rumbling of the ship passing through quiet waters.

CHAPTER ELEVEN

Day Thirty, New York City

ODD HOW THINGS were exactly the same as he'd left them. Well, not *quite* the same. Theo was still very much unemployed and no closer to establishing contact with his parents. They knew he was back in the city since he'd gone by Morgan Greywater to drop off some files he had found in his home office. Of course, they hadn't come to see him, nor had he asked to see them. But there was no way the receptionist hadn't alerted them to his presence in the hospital for the brief thirty seconds this exchange had taken.

What had shocked him, however, had been his colleagues reaching out when they heard about his being back. One of the senior doctors he'd worked with had come jogging out of the building to talk to him at his car. She'd assured him how they understood the pressure he'd been under and that it would have got to a lesser person far sooner. That none of them resented him for leaving, regardless of what he might have heard from the rumour mill.

Something inside Theo had lifted at her words, setting him free of a burden he hadn't been aware he'd been carrying around all this time. The people he'd feared he'd disappointed most had understood why he'd left. Or rather that he hadn't meant to leave in the way he had, but he'd cracked under the pressure of the neverending work and the constantly moving goalposts.

Until that moment, he'd avoided thinking about the future or his place in the world. But the longer he sat idle, the more he realised he needed to do something. Wanted to be a part of something bigger than himself—just not the way his parents had imagined it. The cruise, as much as it hurt to think about it, had shown him how he could make a contribution and use his skills without feeling as if the world was caving in on him.

Theo had got lost, but the last month had shown him there was a way forward. He just needed to figure himself out.

'I'm glad you seem more relaxed,' Angela had said as a goodbye, and her words were still rolling around in his head days later as he sat in this café with a coffee, waiting for a familiar mop of brown hair to appear.

Only apparently Amelie had something else in mind, because when she plonked down on the seat opposite him with her own coffee, her hair sparkled with a deep red colour.

'Can't believe you made me come all the way to New York,' were the first words out of her mouth in weeks, and Theo couldn't help but laugh. It was very much like his sister to start a conversation like that. No preamble. It calmed some of his nerves because he wasn't quite sure *why* she wanted to speak to him.

There were many possible reasons. They were siblings and had grown much closer over their adult years, with the somewhat shared burden of their parents' expectations. They still hadn't really spoken about the cruise and what it had been like to fill in for her. Though if Theo had to guess, there was only one topic that would interest Amelie enough to make her come all the way to New York.

It was also the one thing—one person—he *didn't* want to talk about. In fact, he would much rather go to his parents' place right now and face the music there than sit here and have this conversation. But he knew he needed to have it.

As he'd promised Catalina, he'd managed to stay out of her way—finally snagging a cabin for himself after confiding in Dr Chen. He'd caught glimpses of her at the clinic now and then, though she'd moved around so fast, the message was clear as day: she preferred for him to stay out of her life.

And part of him also wanted to know how Catalina had been. If she was okay. If her life was progressing exactly how she'd hoped it would. Maybe a bit ambitious to expect changes in the span of two weeks, but Theo couldn't help it. Not when the reason he'd walked away from her rather than bury himself inside her for the rest of his life was to ensure she could have the future she wanted. Because being with him would have just traded one cage for another—replacing the awareness of her parents' disinterest in her with the undue scrutiny he knew his significant other would face.

One couldn't avoid it. Except if you were Amelie. Somehow, his sister had untangled herself from everything, and he wasn't sure how she'd done it.

'I didn't make you do anything. You're the one who texted me a time and a place with no other context. A part of me thought this might be an assassination plot.'

Not entirely true. He *wished* it was that rather than what he knew was about to happen. Theo had no idea how much Amelie knew about what had happened between him and Catalina. They were best friends, so he assumed she'd told her a lot. But Amelie was also his sister and maybe didn't *want* to know all the intimate details about her brother helping her best friend lose her virginity—and catching feelings in the process.

'Right, because you were absolutely going to come to Chicago to have a chat with me if I asked you? Even though it's not like you're doing much these days.' Amelie levelled a glare at him.

Theo shrugged. 'There is an invention called the telephone. People use it to communicate with each other over a long distance without having to travel. Did you consider making use of that?'

'Ha-ha, I'm glad you found your sense of humour again. Of course I would have called you if I thought you'd actually pick up the phone.' She paused to look him up and down. 'Ah, you would have picked up. But then I would have had to figure out your prolonged silences over the phone without seeing you. Which was more of a challenge than coming here.'

'How is the hunt for a residency going? Decide on a specialty yet?' he asked, hoping he'd hit the right tone of concerned brother showing an interest in his sister's career rather than the blatant deflection tactic it was.

Amelie's eyes narrowed with a dangerous spark, and he knew she wasn't going to bite. 'That's none of your business, brother. Unless you want me asking a similar question.' She paused, leaning back in her chair and crossing her arms in front of her chest. 'Actually, that's not a bad idea. I'll let you decide what we want to talk about: Catalina or *your* work.'

Theo's stomach tumbled at the mention of the two things in his life that were in complete disarray. Ironic how they also seemed to be the only two things in his life that had ever mattered to him. He'd been adrift before the cruise, thinking of nothing except the next day. Working on the ship—as mundane as the work had been most of the time—had anchored him with a new purpose. Something to hang on to.

And then Catalina had upended it all by making him want more. Teaching him he wasn't just defined by his last name or his achievements. They'd learned the lesson together, choosing to do things because they wanted to rather than living up to ideals or expectations.

Now it was all gone. Theo was drifting again, but this time it was of his own making. He was choosing to be directionless because it was easier than dealing with the storm inside him. Picking up the pieces Catalina had knocked loose simply by being her. Not dealing with how much he *wanted* her to bring such chaos into his life.

'Amelie, I know you mean well…but there's nothing to discuss. I went by the hospital the other day, and I was fine. No discomfort, no triggers. Nothing.' He crossed his arms, then quickly uncrossed them when Amelie's eyes dropped downward. His body language wasn't exactly saying, *I'm totally fine with all this.*

'Fair, but you didn't go inside the hospital. You just went to the lobby, dropped off some stuff, and maybe someone saw you. Definitely not someone with the power to crush your career the way our parents could.'

She wrinkled her nose at the mention of their parents, though something else gave Theo pause.

'How do you know all of this? Did you talk to someone?'

She'd only arrived in New York City a few hours ago. How had she been able to recap something he hadn't told her this accurately?

Amelie scoffed. 'Please, brother. If you are anything, it's predictable. That's why our dear parents put everything on you and were happy enough to let me slide into obscurity. It also means I know exactly what you'll do at any given moment.'

Something about her words grated, and he knew it had to be a childish sibling rivalry making him bristle at his sister's claims. He couldn't help but rise to the challenge—prove her wrong—so he said, 'I bet you didn't see the thing between Catalina and me happening.'

It sounded *way* too braggy, and the moment he said it pain unfurled in his chest, pushing him into instant regret.

'Why did—I shouldn't have said that,' he blurted out almost immediately.

But Amelie was already grinning, eyes sparkling with far too familiar mischief. 'Actually, I did. Like, it was ridiculous how easily you two fell over each other. And I didn't even do much, other than say, "Stay away from her". Which, by the way, was such an obvious piece of bait, but you gobbled it whole.'

She sounded far too pleased with herself, and Theo would be annoyed if his entire brain power wasn't occupied with interpreting her words.

'You did this on purpose?'

His sister gave him a sheepish shrug. 'I wasn't as discouraging as you might have interpreted from my words.'

No, that couldn't be right. How had she—?

'Even your ankle? The accident?'

Amelie's eyes widened, and she let out a laugh loud enough to draw attention towards their table. 'What? No! My God, you think I would— Theo, I'm whimsical, but even I wouldn't risk a permanent injury just to get my best friend laid. No, when I realised I couldn't go, and you were conveniently out of work, that's when the plan came together.'

'And the plan was what? To "get your best friend laid"?' The words tasted like ash in his mouth. He knew it was a ridiculous oversimplification of what they'd shared on the cruise, though now he wasn't certain how much Amelie knew. Had Catalina told her everything?

His sister's expression softened, sending a stab through his chest. She definitely knew enough.

'I wanted you out of New York for a bit. Away from our parents. Give you some perspective on what's out there. You both needed that.'

Real feelings. The words bounced against Theo, looking for a way under his skin. And he felt a pull from within him, wanting to answer the call. Give in to those real feelings even as he said, 'There was nothing. We took things too far, but the agreement was always that things had to end after the cruise.'

The remaining days on the ship had been agony. But throughout it all, Theo had kept telling himself that it was always meant to play out like that. Catalina had just had her first experience with anyone, and anyway, he was wrapped up in so much drama. Dragging her into this—confessing his enduring feelings—wouldn't be fair to her.

'Why, though?' Amelie leant forward, elbows coming down on the table between them.

He shook his head, confused. 'What do you mean?'

'Why contain it to the cruise alone?' She huffed out a laugh. 'I have watched you slyly moon over my best friend for, what, five years now? And yeah, at the beginning I was annoyed. Like, get your own friends to moon over. But then I realised Catalina is one of the most amazing people on the planet, and if I were so inclined I would have mooned over her, too. Sadly, I'm straight.' She let out a sigh dramatic enough to cut some of the tension between them. 'You finally *got* her, Theo. And it became blatantly apparent to me over the course of this cruise that this is more to both of you than some silly forbidden-fruit crush. Why are you letting go of it all?'

'I don't have her and never had. This was designed to be casual. A...favour wrapped in companionship.' He felt dirty even as he said it—reducing what they'd shared to nothing more than a deal. But how else was he supposed to protect her?

'I know it was more for her, and I'm pretty certain that you aren't being completely honest about your feelings, either.'

Amelie examined him, and he forced himself not to squirm under her probing gaze.

It was more for her? So she did talk to Amelie about everything?

'I can't let her—she doesn't know what she'd be agreeing to, being with me right now. You know our parents have probably already blacklisted me from every single noteworthy medical institute in the States.'

To his surprise, Amelie simply shrugged. As if all he'd laid out for her didn't matter.

'Our parents are maniacs, and I'm sure they did some damage control in the background. But what does it matter if you are blacklisted at every noteworthy institute? Didn't stop you from working as a doctor on the cruise, did it?'

'But that was a cruise. I can't spend the rest of my life doing that.'

'I mean, you could if you've fallen in love with the lifestyle. But that's not what I mean.' She shook her head, and her expression relaxed into an uncharacteristic softness. 'There are plenty of hospitals out there that will hire you on the spot, no questions asked. Plenty of places where the influence of our parents is non-existent. Hell, there are even institutes like Attano Memorial, which have an active rivalry with anything Morgan related.'

Theo's eyes widened at that. 'Is that why you went there? Some kind of corporate espionage?'

'No, nothing of the sort. You think I know anything about our parents' business? But…' She paused, mulling his comments over. 'I guess *you* know enough that people might just hire you to get some insider info on the Morgan empire. Something to consider.'

Was it really so simple? Theo couldn't believe it. His entire life—his career—had been laid out the moment he'd finished high school. College, med school, internship, residency—they'd all been selected ahead of time for him. Given to him like a blessing, with the promise of how many great things he would do. How he was now responsible for the continued success of Morgan Greywater.

He had never considered anything else. Not until he'd walked out of the emergency room, never to go back. Not until… Catalina. Working side by side with her on the most mundane cases imaginable had unlocked a deep yearning within him. One he'd tried to smother over those two weeks, too scared of what might happen if he let it go on.

The fantasy of *what-if* was so close, he could almost grasp it.

When he remained silent, Amelie reached out and put a hand on his arm. 'I think you've been so wrapped up in talk of legacy and carrying on the name and whatnot that you've never stopped to consider what you want. Are noteworthy institutes even something you want? Or would you be happy just to open up a clinic somewhere? Live your best life?'

He had thought about it, but only in the quiet moments. How refreshing it had been to go to the ship's clinic every morning and see what the day brought in. Even the more stressful days had still been such an improvement on the pressures of the ER at Morgan Greywater.

He had considered it, yes. But… 'Only more reason why Catalina shouldn't associate with me. I might not want the big career, but she's choosing her residency spot, and she should do that without any other consideration than herself.'

Amelie let go of his arm and leant back. 'I'm pretty sure she's done with the ambitious life. It's brought her more trouble than pleasure. But I think you know that.'

Theo was surprised that he did. So much of her ambition and self-worth had been driven by the need to gain her family's approval and love, only for them to hold her at arm's length. The trip had been the ultimate tribute to rejecting a life of chasing those things which wouldn't bring her happiness.

Theo stared at the dregs of his coffee. The silence between them was no longer heavy but clarifying. Maybe for the first time in his life, he understood what it meant to want something without being told he should. Not because it was expected or strategic, but because *he* wanted it. Not the name. Not the empire. Just Catalina—her laugh, her chaos, her ridiculous way of turning everything into something fun.

And maybe that was the problem. He hadn't just walked away from a relationship—he'd walked away from *wanting*. From the one person who had asked nothing of him except honesty. He'd called it sacrifice, claimed it was for her sake, but the truth was simpler and far more cowardly: he'd been terrified he might no longer be a person worthy of her love.

He stared at his hands. How many times had he held her with them? How often had he longed to? When he recalled the way she'd looked at him that last night, the impossible tenderness, he realised he'd been helpless from the beginning. Even if he'd planned the exit perfectly, it wouldn't have made the absence easier.

'What if she's moved on?' he blurted, the words slipping out before he could crush them under his tongue.

Amelie's mouth curled, but not in the way he was prepared for—there was no smugness in it, just a painful kind of fondness.

'I'm honestly not sure she can. She's an all-or-nothing person. Like someone else at this table.' She sipped her coffee, eyeing him over the rim. 'You know, when she got back from the cruise, she called me at two in the morning. Didn't say a word for the first couple of minutes, just sobbed. You've kind of pissed me off with this whole thing, actually. You're not using your head.' She set the cup down. 'I think she's hoping you'll get over yourself and call her.'

He stood so abruptly that Amelie startled, nearly knocking over her half-empty cup. She raised an eyebrow, lips already twitching into a smirk. 'You're going to do it, aren't you?'

Theo blinked, still feeling the aftershock of his decision. 'Do what?'

'A grand gesture!' She slapped the table, looking so gleeful he almost reconsidered. 'You're going to run after her right now, like in the movies. Only please, for the love of God, do not try to get through TSA with a bouquet. It's embarrassing for everyone involved, and Catalina doesn't even like flowers.'

He pressed his lips together. The idea of running—towards, not away—had never occurred to him in such a literal sense.

'I don't have a plan. I just need to see her.' Even as he said it, something in him clicked into alignment. He needed to see Catalina. Not for closure, not to beg forgiveness, but because he was afraid if he waited much longer, the space she'd carved out of him would calcify. Become permanent.

He couldn't let that happen.

CHAPTER TWELVE

Day Thirty, Chicago

'AND WITH THIS, you're all set to go.' Catalina pressed a small box into the woman's hands, giving her a smile as she thanked Catalina and hurried out of the exam room.

Catalina slumped back when the door behind her closed. It had been a week and a bit since she had returned to Chicago. Most of the time she'd spent hiding away in her room so that she could avoid Amelie and her inevitable probing questions about Theo. Though part of her was certain her best friend already knew everything. She just didn't know how.

Theo wouldn't tell her anything, would he?

Just thinking his name sent a painful flutter through her, and she pushed all of those thoughts away. Needing a distraction was also the reason why she was at the free clinic run by her former hospital, Alexander Attano Memorial. Dr Santos-Henderson, the lead of the clinic, hadn't asked any questions when Catalina had shown up, volunteering her time. Anything to get out of the apartment and, more importantly, out of her head.

If she didn't, she would no doubt do something foolish like break down and call Theo. Or worse, book a flight to New York and track him down like some lovesick maniac. Because that was where she was now—pining. *Still.* He'd broken her heart into pieces, confirming her worst fears in the process, and she couldn't get him out of her head. Couldn't scrub the ghost of his touch from her skin, no matter how hard she tried.

As if he lived just below the surface, where it would be the most painful to extract him.

A knock sounded on the door, making her sit up straight. 'Yes?'

Emma Santos-Henderson stuck her head in. 'That's the last one on the list,' she said with a warm smile that set Catalina at ease.

During her internship at the hospital, she'd spent more time with her husband, the head of oncology, than with Dr Santos-Henderson, though her time in the free clinic had been one of her favourite times here. Something about knowing her skills were helping the people who needed them most sat right with her.

Was that maybe what she should do? On top of the broken heart, she could add a professional crisis, given she was nowhere closer to figuring it out. Another thing the cruise should have helped with. Now that she was back, Catalina could safely say the entire thing had been a complete bust.

Instead of hooking up with some random but cute guy, she was stuck with her head and her heart wrapped around the ultimate cute guy who didn't want to have her. Somehow it had turned out the opposite of empowering.

'Okay, thanks for letting me know.' Shaking her head, Catalina got off her chair and shut down the computer before leaving the exam room.

With the clinic being as small as it was, it didn't have a dedicated staffroom. Instead, they used a small cupboard behind the front desk to stash their personal belongings during the day. When Catalina opened it, only one other bag hung there along with her own. Turning around with her tote slung over her shoulder, she looked towards Emma. 'Same time tomorrow?'

The other woman gave her a small smile. 'Sure. We're not in a position to turn down any help here.'

Catalina was about to leave when Emma chuckled, and the sound was such an odd surprise that she stopped in her tracks and turned back.

'What's got you in such a good mood?' she asked, feeling as if she'd missed out on the joke. Emma wasn't a particularly stone-faced person, but during their collaboration she'd never approached Catalina with anything more than friendly professionalism. Had she ever heard the woman laugh like that?

'Ah, I said the same thing to my husband years ago when I first wandered in here. Funny how it's come full circle.' She laughed again and then her lips closed in a wistful smile. 'This clinic used to be his side project, but when we came back to Chicago, I spent more time here until I became the natural choice to lead it. Not where I saw my career going, but exactly what I needed, and still do.'

A million questions popped into Catalina's mind. Mark Henderson used to take care of this clinic? Knowing how much research he did, how many papers he wrote and the groundbreaking work he did as a surgeon, she couldn't even imagine where he found time for anything else. How did he stay married—happily at that, going by Emma's soft expression as she spoke of her spouse?

Theo was a Mark Henderson-type person. Or at least he had been before he'd walked out of his job. Now he was lost in what to do next, so unsure of where life would take him he couldn't imagine sharing even a part of it with Catalina.

Not that she could do much talking on that front. She was spending her days at the free clinic because she equally did not know what to do with her life. What gave her the confidence to know she could figure it out while still being with Theo and taking him into consideration?

The fury at his actions had lessened to a low simmer of indignation—one which had been tested every single day since. On the first day back home, she'd woken up with a small voice in her head, asking her if Theo had been right. Was she able to pick her path forward just based on what she wanted, or would she automatically compromise because of him? Seek his approval in her next step, the way she'd always had with her parents?

Catalina had operated like that for so long, a part of her believed she didn't know how to do things that weren't focused on chasing approval.

'If you don't have anywhere urgent to be, would you like to sit with me for a moment?' Emma asked, snapping Catalina out of her thoughts.

She followed Emma's gaze, trained on the chair Catalina had been clinging to with her hands as she'd gone down the mental spiral.

'Oh…' The metal legs scraped against the linoleum flooring as she pulled it out and plopped down with a sound rather lacking in any grace.

Emma continued to smile at her, though something now lurked beneath it. She didn't let Catalina guess for long before she said, 'As much as I love having you here, why aren't you out there looking for a residency spot? Most of your peers from earlier in the year are already in their residency programs.'

Oh, good. Another person to disappoint with her indecision. She hadn't even thought that Emma Santos-Henderson would have noticed, yet here she was, struggling to come up with the words to explain why she was volunteering at a free clinic instead of building her career just like everyone else in her peer group.

Except there was no judgement in Emma's gaze, as Catalina had expected. And it was the gentleness that broke through Catalina's reserves, breaking the dam and letting the truth come spilling out of her.

'When we finished up here, Amelie—Dr Morgan—suggested doing something fun for the summer before we go into our specialisations. So we signed up as medical staff for a cruise through the Mediterranean. Only, a few days before we were shipping out, Amelie broke her ankle and so she asked her brother to sub in for her. A brother who, I'm annoyed to say, I've been crushing on since we met in med school. Part of me thinks Amelie did this on purpose, because that would be just like her. But she clearly hadn't thought any of this through because now I'm here, an absolute mess because of Theo.'

The words wouldn't stop coming, and as Catalina went on, Emma's eyebrow wandered further up. When she stopped, it was almost at the other woman's hairline. Silence stretched between them—long enough for Catalina to regret her emotional outburst—but then Emma said, 'Dr Theodore Morgan went on a cruise as medical staff? Of all the things he was rumoured to be doing, this one wasn't on anyone's list.'

Now it was Catalina's turn to be surprised. 'You know Theo?'

Emma's smile was gentle. 'Everyone knows the Morgan Greywater Institute, including who is currently attached to the highly prestigious emergency room. Theodore Morgan isn't on nearly as many front covers as Mark, but I think that says more about how much my husband likes to see his face out there.' She chuckled before she continued. 'It set tongues wagging when Theodore left the way he did. Not that I'm entirely surprised he did. The job is far more pressure than one person alone can handle, and being under the watchful eye of the Morgan Greywater Foundation can't help. There's been talk going around in the medical community that its biggest priority is preserving its good name rather than caring for the mental health of its doctors.'

Catalina stared at Emma, absorbing the new pieces of information. Some of it sounded familiar. The pressure of the job and how the Morgans were more concerned about their image matched the things Amelie had always said about her parents. It was the reason she wanted nothing to do with the dynasty and had chosen a different path.

'I wonder if Theo still has the option of a different path,' she said quietly, more to herself.

But Emma picked up on it anyway. 'What do you mean?'

'Amelie—she came here to be with me. Her parents had her entire internship path sorted out. But she said while she loves medicine, she doesn't like what her parents are asking of her or her brother. But she's free-spirited like that, unlike Theo. I think he grew up with all this expectation on his shoulders and now that he's walked away from it all, he doesn't know what to do.' Amelie rarely spoke about her parents, but when she did, their controlling nature came across without a doubt. Something Catalina could understand. Her parents had been controlling, too. Not by demanding she did certain things, but rather by withholding things from her—affection and love—when she didn't meet their arbitrary threshold. And of course she'd never been able to find the right things to do or to say when the goalposts moved at random.

'I'm not going to pretend to know what Theodore Morgan's journey of self-discovery has been like, but we all carry some things with us, for better or for worse. For years, I let some unprocessed things from my family's side stop me from making choices I needed to make for myself. The same can be true for our loved ones. Sometimes we think we know what's best for them, and that's how we act.' She paused when Catalina looked at her with wide eyes. 'Something I said resonating with you?'

A lump appeared in Catalina's throat, and she tried to swallow it down. Her voice still sounded rough when she replied. 'Most of my choices came from a place of wanting to impress my parents. As the middle child out of eight, I got the bare minimum of attention from them, and only ever when they thought I was excelling. And so of course I made that my entire personality until very recently.'

Why was she telling Emma Santos-Henderson any of this? Of all the people to spill her guts to, the doctor leading up the free clinic where she spent some of her time seemed like a strange choice. But her eyes remained kind—so did her smile—and Catalina felt encouraged to continue.

'I understand now that I was never going to get what I wanted that way. Like, I'm a doctor. I've done the few hours of mandatory psychology training sufficient to recognise this dynamic as toxic.'

'But it's one thing to recognise it and an entirely different thing to break it,' Emma said, getting an emphatic nod from Catalina in return.

'Right. And while I loved doing my internship here, and I'm grateful to have made the cut, I've realised this was just another move to please people who don't see me for who I am. I thought an internship at a big-name hospital after graduating top of my class from a respected med school would net me what I want. But it hasn't. And the cruise… It was my way to break free from expectations. Reclaim some space inside myself. And it worked, because I enjoyed myself for the first time in so long. Sure, the work was often easy and sometimes monotonous, but there's nothing wrong with that, right? If I enjoy it…'

Throughout the cruise, this had been eating at the back of her mind—whenever her entire thought process wasn't occupied with Theo and the riot of feelings he inspired in her.

'Nothing wrong with that. I thought once I wanted the same career Mark has, but then I found my calling here in the free clinic. If you found something that makes you happy, go for it.'

Catalina's brain grappled with Emma's words, so casually given, yet their impact undeniable.

But before she could say anything, the other woman continued. 'It sounds like you've made peace with never getting the recognition you want from your parents. Meanwhile, Theodore has been raised to do this one thing, and has both the recognition and the responsibility that comes with it. Or had it until he walked out. It's like you are different sides of the same coin.'

'How do you know so much about him?' Emma's words were way too accurate for someone who had never interacted with Theo. Had she formed this opinion from Catalina's emotional ramble alone?

'The medical community is an odd one. Because of Mark's position, he often rubs shoulders with the chiefs of these places, trading pleasantries and whatnot.' She waved a hand in front of her. 'Through him, I've met Sinclair Morgan a few times, and the only thing he drones on about is his family's reputation and the legacy they're creating. I'm not going to judge anyone trying to escape such an environment, but I do understand caution. It's a sticky web to untangle, with so many eyes on him. Even I heard about his exit, so it's more than likely he's spending his days now dodging scrutiny.'

Catalina had to admit that even though she understood difficult family dynamics, the political side of medicine was foreign to her, and would remain so. With the clarity she'd gained on the cruise—and through this conversation, surprisingly—the picture of her future became clearer. The high-octane environment of a top-performing institute wasn't where she could see herself. No, the pace of the cruise had been exactly what she wanted professionally—and she had more than enough training to do that.

Maybe this is *genuinely why Theo walked away.*

The thought fluttered in on silent wings, yet

somehow performed a crash landing—making it impossible to think about anything else. Could it really be…?

The man she'd got to know on the cruise wasn't uncaring. Quite the opposite. What if he really had walked away because he cared? So much so that he couldn't bear the idea of her giving things up for him. If Emma knew all these things about him, so must many other people. Enough for him to genuinely worry about what kind of impact her association with him would have on her further training.

Catalina hadn't believed it, but now it looked more like she was the one who hadn't known enough about the situation to judge his actions. He'd been trying to protect her in the only way he knew how.

The ache in her chest shifted—no less painful but different.

All this time, she'd thought she wanted to be chosen. That if someone looked her in the eye and said she was enough, all those years of silence from her parents would dissolve. But Theo *had* looked at her like that. Held her like she mattered, and still she waited for more.

He had chosen her, but she had been too wrapped up in her own version of wanting to be chosen to see him.

Her breath rattled out of her, and she scrubbed her palms down her thighs as she met Emma's gaze. Something new stirred just behind her ribs. Not certainty or hope. But the pull of something worth chasing.

If she could muster the courage.

CHAPTER THIRTEEN

Day Thirty-three, Chicago

COURAGE ONLY CAME to Catalina three days later, and it came in the form of a shirtless paramedic on a TV commercial. Well, not really, but that was how she would later go on to recall the story. What actually happened was her phone pinging and jolting her out of her half-sleep to the picture of the muscled-up paramedic on her television.

Groping for her phone, she squinted as the too-high brightness burned into her retinas for a second too long before the phone adjusted to its dim surroundings. On the top of her list of notifications was a message from Amelie. No, an email. Since when did her best friend send her emails?

When she tapped on it, it contained nothing but a blue link to a news site. The words *Morgan*, *Greywater* and *Emergency Room* jumped out at her from the URL. With her thumb hovering over the link, Catalina blinked several times.

She pressed, and the screen loaded, sluggish on

her building's mediocre Wi-Fi. The article banner was a high-contrast photo of the Morgan Greywater Institute—a slab of glass and steel, severe as a confession. The headline read: *Morgan Greywater Appoints New Head of Emergency Medicine*. Underneath, another line: *With the sudden vacancy, Sinclair Morgan lauds the appointment of Dr Priya Deshpande as the future of patient-centred trauma care.*

Catalina's eyes searched the first paragraphs—her brain assembling and reassembling the context, looking for Theo's name. She expected a mention of the predecessor, maybe a sentence or two about his 'sabbatical' or 'pioneering work'. Instead, there was only a brisk summary of Dr Deshpande's accolades, her years of service at a different Greywater hospital, and a cloying quote from the patriarch himself about 'family legacy and renewal'.

Theo's name did not once appear.

It was as if he'd never occupied the role, never helmed the ER. As if he had been scrubbed from its institutional memory in the span of one cruise. Yet his father still had the gall to talk about legacy with a bright smile when the pressure of that had broken his son—the man who had given everything to preserve the reputation of the Institute. Who had *lost* everything because of it, too.

Including her. She hadn't believed him when he'd told her about his reservations. She'd assumed it to be an excuse because it had been what she'd heard so often in her life from her parents. And then from herself whenever she failed to get the acknowledgement she wanted.

But what she and Theo had wasn't about acknowledgement or attention or anything this tenuous. It had *never* been about that. How had she ever reduced it to just this? Okay, yes, the entire cruise had been designed to get her laid, as a first step to reclaiming her life and her confidence and finally getting to choose the things she wanted to do.

But what if those things were Theo? She hadn't even stopped to consider that.

'Damn you, Amelie,' Catalina muttered as she climbed off the couch with her phone in her hand.

She shouldn't have walked out on Theo, and it had only taken her two weeks and a bit to figure that one out. Great. That wasn't a long time, was it? Was there a chance if she booked a flight to New York right now that he'd be horrified to see her, having somehow already moved on to the next iteration of his picture-perfect life?

Because Catalina needed to tell him she'd made up her mind. That she would be happier with him and working in a free clinic for the rest of her life than living without him and pursuing a high-powered career that would only lead her down a path where unscrupulous people could erase her existence in flashy news articles the moment she did something they didn't like. Where she would end up replacing the approval of one person with another without ever considering what she wanted.

Life was too short to chase unattainable glory when the possibility of a lifetime with Theo was right in front of her. If he would meet her there. There was the chance he was dead set on his impression that associating with him would ruin her, when actually the opposite was true.

But she needed to tell him. Over and over again, if that was what it took.

She dialled Amelie before she'd formed a plan, the phone ringing three, four, five times before her best friend's voicemail kicked in. Catalina paced the length of the apartment, one hand pressed to her temple, the other cradling the device as she waited for the beep.

'Amelie. I know what you did. I know—' Her voice cracked, and she stopped, staring at the peeling laminate of the kitchenette as if it could explain to her the depth of her own idiocy. 'You sent me that link because you're an evil mastermind, and also possibly a romantic villain, and I swear to God I'm going to pay you back for this.'

She slumped against the counter, the late-afternoon sun throwing a wobbly rectangle across the debris field of her living room. The tote bag from yesterday's shift lay crumpled where she'd dropped it.

'I'm not mad,' she said, more to herself than

Amelie, 'but just so you know, I'm about to make the single most impulsive decision of my adult life, and if this blows up in my face, I'm blaming you for the next five years.' Why five years? She wasn't sure, but it seemed like an appropriate timeframe to hold a grudge.

She inhaled, steadying. 'I'm in love with Theo. And I need to get that through to him so he can stop being all perfect and self-sacrificing and whatever other heroic things go on in his mind.' Catalina paused, staring at the clock hanging on the wall. Could she get out of here tonight and see him? She had to try. 'I'm going to fix this. I'm going to New York. If you have any last-minute advice, text me, but only if it's not "Go get a grip, Catalina, you're being ridiculous".' Because if she was being honest, this was the most Amelie thing to do.

She hung up, finished packing her bag in a tornado of limbs, and yanked open her apartment door with an impatient flourish—only to nearly collide with the man she'd planned to hunt down across the country.

Theo stood in the doorway, hand raised, inches from rapping on her door. He wore no coat, only a cable-knit navy sweater stretched over his shoulders, as if he'd left in a rush. His hair was mussed, his shoes scuffed and everything about him was imperfect—unlike Theo and yet somehow exactly how she remembered him.

For a second, neither of them spoke. The silence grew—awkward, electric, full of unsaid things.

Theo dropped his arm and stared at her, as if he couldn't believe what he was seeing. 'Hi,' he said, his voice cracking on the word.

She stared at him, heart hammering so loud she was sure it would rattle the windows. 'What are you doing here?' In her shock, the words came out sharper than she meant.

He looked down at his shoes. 'I didn't want to call. I thought you'd just—' He broke off, mouth twisting. 'Honestly, I wasn't sure if you'd want to see me.'

'I didn't want to see you—' she started, and his face crumpled—actually crumpled, as if her words were a fist. 'No, that's not right. I meant I didn't think you would want to see me. I was about to walk out my own door and hunt you down like a crazed stalker, Theo, so maybe let's call it even.' She winced, breathless. 'I mean, I was going to New York, and now you're here, and I—' She broke off, closing her eyes. The world felt as if it was buzzing, her hands trembling so hard she gripped the doorframe for support.

Theo blinked, then his mouth did a twitchy half-smile, the kind that used to surface only when she'd said something that genuinely surprised him. It was so familiar it made her knees tremble. 'Really?'

She nodded, swallowing around the lump in

her throat. He was *here*. Theo had beaten her to it and appeared in front of her like an apparition. She wanted to reach out, throw herself at him and bury her face in his neck. But she couldn't—not yet. There were still things to discuss, even if her heart was telling her these were no more than details. He was here, and that was all that counted.

'Really,' she forced out, echoing him. 'I was about to leave and tell you that I was wrong not to listen and—'

Theo stepped forward. The scent of sandalwood hit her first, and then his arms came around her, pulling her against him in an embrace she hadn't realised she'd been longing for all this time. A shiver ran down her spine when his hands found their way up her back, almost lifting her off the floor.

'I won't have you apologising for even a second. This is all my fault, so I'll have none of that from you.' He straightened himself enough to look at her, and what she saw glittering in those eyes stole the breath from her lungs. 'I'm sorry I pushed you away. I thought I was protecting you from my influence—letting you have the career you always wanted without having to explain who I am. I'd never forgive myself if I was the reason you couldn't follow your dreams.'

Her chest tightened when his voice wobbled, and she shook her head before he could continue. 'No, I understand now. I didn't on the cruise, but now… I get it. What your family can do if they disagree with you. How they all but erased you from their history. For what? Wanting to live your life on your own terms?' Catalina still reeled from the realisation. 'I get you wanted to protect me from this. But I just—the life you think I wanted, it's not real. I don't want something where I can't be with you, Theo. I love you.'

The confession seemed to detonate in the narrow hallway, expanding to fill the space between them. For a heartbeat, Theo simply stared at her. Then something radiant and reckless lit behind his eyes, and he closed the small distance between them, his mouth finding hers in a kiss that expressed his feelings the way his words couldn't.

She gasped, but not from surprise. It was oxygen after having drowned for weeks. She pressed herself up on her toes, tangled her hands in the hair at his nape, and let herself be gathered. His mouth was greedy and his arms a cage, but she had never felt more free. The air between them crackled with the aftershock of her words, and Theo's trembling hand cupped her jaw as if to keep the moment from running away.

When he finally broke for air, his forehead dropped to hers, and she felt the shudder of his exhale against her lips.

'Say it again,' he whispered, voice frayed at the edges. 'Please.'

She laughed, heart beating in her throat, but she

didn't hesitate. 'I love you, Theo.' Each word a stone thrown through the window of her old life.

His hands were everywhere—her cheeks, her hair, her waist—and his own confession barrelled out of him, helpless and raw: 'I love you, too. I have for longer than you know. God, Cat…'

She smiled against his cheek. 'I know now.'

They stood there, suspended in each other's gravity, until he caught her chin and pulled her back to eye level. 'You need to understand, though. I meant what I said about the fallout. I may never work at a big hospital again. I have no idea what's coming next. And I don't want you to regret this, Catalina. Not a year from now, not ever.'

His voice was raw, so unguarded it nearly broke her. But for the first time, she didn't feel the sharp reflex of competitiveness. Rather, a warm feeling spread through her. She reached for his face, thumbing the faint stubble along his jaw, and felt the ache in her chest expand into something fierce and shining.

'I don't want any of the things I used to want, Theo—if I ever truly wanted them for myself anyway. If I had wanted them, I would have stayed on the path. But I'm off it—and I like the view from here. I don't care where we end up, as long as we're together. I don't need anything fancy. What we did on the cruise, working one-on-one with people—it was the best experience I've ever had. So if you tell me we'll be cruise doctors for now, sign me up. As long as it's with you.'

He let out a shaky laugh and buried his head in her shoulder, breathing her in.

'You know, I had this whole speech planned out on the plane. How I was going to stand here and tell you I love you but that I couldn't be selfish enough to ask you to choose me. But now you've upstaged me.'

Catalina laughed—full and unguarded. Happy. 'Upstaged you? I *was* about to cross state lines in your honour. You're lucky I didn't show up at your door holding a boom box.'

Theo pulled back just enough to look at her, brows lifted. 'I don't think you'll ever stop surprising me, Cat.'

'I contain multitudes…' She shrugged, each word they exchanged lifting her spirit. This was happening. This was really happening.

'You do,' he murmured, brushing a strand of hair from her cheek with a touch that made her breath catch. 'And I want a front-row seat to all of them.'

Theo took her hands and held them between his, the weight of everything they weren't saying behind the simple touch. 'Let's figure it out. The future. I don't care where or how. Clinic, cruise ship, cabin in the woods—I'll start googling job boards tonight if you want. As long as I get to build it with you.'

A lump caught in her throat again, but this time it didn't hurt. 'No more running?'

He shook his head. 'Only toward you.'

And then he kissed her again, slow and certain this time, sealing the beginning of everything.

* * * * *

If you enjoyed this story, check out these other great reads from Luana DaRosa

Falling for the GP Next Door
Faking It with the Doctor Prince
Falling for Her Miami Rival
Hot Nights with the Arctic Doc

All available now!

Get up to 4 Free Books!

We'll send you 2 free books from each series you try PLUS a free Mystery Gift.

Both the **Harlequin Presents** and **Harlequin Medical Romance** series feature exciting stories of passion and drama.

YES! Please send me 2 FREE novels from Harlequin Presents or Harlequin Medical Romance and my FREE gift (gift is worth about $10 retail). I may cancel anytime by emailing ReaderServiceInfo@Harlequin.com or by calling 1-800-873-8635.If I don't cancel, I will receive 6 brand-new larger-print novels every month and be billed just $7.19 each in the U.S., or $7.99 each in Canada, or 4 brand-new Harlequin Medical Romance Larger-Print books every month and be billed just $7.19 each in the U.S. or $7.99 each in Canada. That's a savings of 20% off the cover price! It's quite a bargain! Shipping and handling is just 75¢ per book in the U.S. and $1.75 per book in Canada.* I understand that accepting the free books and gift places me under no obligation to buy anything—they are mine to keep for free no matter what I decide.

Choose one: ☐ **Harlequin Presents Larger-Print** (176/376 BPA G3CD) ☐ **Harlequin Medical Romance** (171/371 BPA G3CD) ☐ **Or Try Both!** (176/376 & 171/371 BPA G3CE)

Name (please print)

Address | Apt. #

City | State/Province | Zip/Postal Code

Email: Please check this box ☐ if you would like to receive newsletters and promotional emails from Harlequin Enterprises ULC and its affiliates. You can unsubscribe anytime.

Mail to the **Harlequin Reader Service:**
IN U.S.A.: P.O. Box 1341, Buffalo, NY 14240-8531
IN CANADA: P.O. Box 603, Fort Erie, Ontario L2A 5X3

Want to explore our other series or interested in ebooks? Visit www.ReaderService.com or call 1-800-873-8635.

*Terms and prices subject to change without notice. Prices do not include sales taxes, which will be charged (if applicable) based on your state or country of residence. Canadian residents will be charged applicable taxes. Offer not valid in Quebec. This offer is limited to one order per household. Books received may not be as shown. Not valid for current subscribers to the Harlequin Presents or Harlequin Medical Romance series. All orders subject to approval. Credit or debit balances in a customer's account(s) may be offset by any other outstanding balance owed by or to the customer. Please allow 4 to 6 weeks for delivery. Offer available while quantities last.

Your Privacy — Your information is being collected by Harlequin Enterprises ULC, operating as Harlequin Reader Service. For a complete summary of the information we collect, how we use this information and to whom it is disclosed, please visit our privacy notice located at https://corporate.harlequin.com/privacy-notice. Notice to California Residents—Under California law, you have specific rights to control and access your data. For more information on these rights and how to exercise them, visit https://corporate.harlequin.com/california-privacy. For additional information for residents of other U.S. states that provide their residents with certain rights with respect to personal data, visit https://corporate.harlequin.com/other-state-residents-privacy-rights.

HPHM2603